R3D GOLIATH

MX Publishing

Other books in the CODE NAME DELTA series:

The Quadrille

One Deadly Souk

The Caribbean Sedition

The Magdalena Gambit

Killing for Profit

Man on Target

The Impostor

A New Kind of War

King of the Slaughtermen

A Honey Smeared Trap

To Know is to Die

The Circumstantial Hitman

The Poisonous Hand

Dead Dog Won't Bite

THE SECRET FILE OF PATRICK COONAN

R3D GOLIATH

Oscar Ortiz

MX Publishing

Book #2 in the CODE NAME DELTA series

RED GOLIATH

Copyright © 2024 by Oscar F. Ortiz

MX Publishing
335 Princess Park Manor, Royal Drive,
London, N11 3GX, United Kingdom

Paperback ISBN: 978-1-80424-425-8
eBook PDF ISBN: 978-1-80424-427-2
eBook ePub ISBN: 978-1-80424-426-5

To my son Alex Francisco,
my dear "Big Guy"

Praise for Red Goliath

AWARDED 5 STARS BY THE ONLINE BOOK CLUB

"Red Goliath, *by Oscar Ortiz, immerses the readers into the complex world of crime and espionage set against the backdrop of Miami's tumultuous history. The protagonist, Agent Delta, undergoes a gripping transformation from a disillusioned operative to a hardened agent, navigating a treacherous landscape of rival gangs and corrupt officials. Delta's internal struggle between duty and morality adds depth to the narrative, prompting thought-provoking questions about justice and individual ethics. The relentless pacing and well-crafted editing make for a thrilling read, earning the book a commendable 5-star rating. I highly recommend it to fans of crime, espionage, and international intrigue for its enthralling plot and meaningful exploration of broader societal themes."*

Veronica Hunter
Reviewer for The Online Book Club.

REPLACING IAN FLEMING WITH ALL THE HONORS

"In times where fiction plays the game in everything to the conventions of "political correctness," where every word is scrutinized with a magnifying glass to avoid annoying those whose mission in life is, after all, to be offended by everything that does not fit in with their single-minded ideology, and their gratifying concept of artistic manifestations and censorship concealed under an excessive zeal for the protection of the spectator and/or the reader, we welcome every new Patrick Coonan novel by author Oscar Ortiz as a darned good alternative. Ortiz seems to insist on replacing Ian Fleming with all the honors, introducing in popular

fiction the adventures of a new antihero of rampant hetero-sexuality, dedicated to the counterintelligence game and the protection of the Free World. Ortiz's series is titled CODE NAME DELTA, its protagonist is named Patrick Coonan, and this is the second book in the collection. Consequently, this author strikes me as an unfiltered Fleming, without distillates, while remaining faithful to the ideology that the late British author abandoned when the 007 stories left behind the Cold War, and ultimately took to large-scale crime and weapons trafficking."

Josep Ferran Valls
Reviewer for Mightier than the Sword.

ESTABLISHING HIS OWN NARRATIVE

"As it usually happens in the detective stories — where every detail is of utmost importance — the passages of this book that we could analyze would be detrimental to the interest of the reader. However, the prose shows once again the catchy first-person narrative style of Oscar Ortiz, who has achieved his own language heavily drawing from the precise rules of the Noir mystery tales, a genre which he dominates quite clearly, proving that, within the so-called Spy thrillers, Ortiz has established himself as one of today's most outstanding exponents."

Luis de la Paz
Literary critic for the Miami newspaper *El Nuevo Herald.*

"A military operation involves deception. Even if you are competent, you must appear incompetent. Even if you are effective, show yourself to be ineffective."

TABLE OF CONTENTS

FOREWORD

(An introduction to The Secret File of Patrick Coonan)

In recent times, the cinematic James Bond has been converted into a "catwalk muscleman" bearing an asphalt face and a propensity for melancholy. To escape from this new "politically correct" version of the character, incapable of being seductive and without any trace of the model developed by Ian Fleming in his novels, there still are few options available. The most obvious one is to review Fleming's books or the films starring Sean Connery and his most popular successors. Another option is the pulp narrative alternative to 007, currently well served by the prolific Cuban American writer Oscar Ortiz. This is the series *Code Name Delta*, featuring Patrick Coonan, a U.S. Rangers' sniper transformed into a clandestine operator for the Quadrille — the sharp counterintelligence unit created by Ret. Special Forces Col. Marlon Berkowitz to safeguard America from all threats. Always with the protracted shadow of the Cold War as the background, which also served as the main setting in the first Bond book written by Fleming. Ortiz's virtues as a novelist can be well-appreciated in all his Patrick Coonan adventures: a concise, direct prose, halfway between the noir mystery genre and the spy thriller; utmost erudition in the different topics dealt with, where one perceives a thorough work of research and the offering to the reader of varied plots that combine investigation, violent death, sexuality, and an uncomfortable background of moral sordidness.

Josep Ferran Valls
Valencia, Spain - Oct. 2022

DRAMATIS PERSONAE

ALEKSEI
Krista Kaminski's bodyguard with whom she plays erotic games behind her husband's back. He is tall, muscular, and always armed.

BERKOWITZ (Marlon)
A.k.a. the Colonel. A former member of the U.S. Special Forces, and Vietnam War veteran. He is the founder and director of operations of the Quadrille. Coonan's chief.

BUCHINSKY (Dave)
A dark, underworld character from Brighton Beach, N.Y. The most blood-thirsty Mafia enforcer on the entire East Coast; also known by the sobriquet The Butcher. Hired by Leo Kaminski to supervise his bodyguards.

COONAN (Patrick)
He is Col. Berkowitz's best eliminator; also, one of his most loyal followers who deserves all his trust. Protagonist of this series. His code name is Delta.

CUEVAS (Rudy)
A small-time crook of Colombian nationality. He is Leo and Krista Kaminski's overseas partner in the operation of floating casinos they are in the process of establishing in the Florida Keys. Cuevas represents a group of Colombian money forgers that traffic in fake U.S. dollars.

INDIO BILLY
Bodyguard of Rudy Cuevas, a Herculean thug of Colombian origin. Works as a team with Rico.

JOHNSON (William)
Alias Bill. He is a jovial, somewhat cynical African American who doesn't take his retirement well. Bill is the official armorer of the Quadrille. After being pensioned off the FBI, Johnson was picked by Col. Berkowitz to head the Armory & the Special Effects Department. He gets along quite well with Pat.

KAMINSKI (Krista)
A worldly woman with a pedantic character. She is as despotic as she is beautiful. Blonde, pale-skinned and the owner of a superb female body of

exuberant curves which she uses to manipulate all men around her. Frivolous and calculating, a true femme fatale if ever there were one.

KAMINSKI (Leonid)

A.k.a. The Sower, one of the local Russian Mafia capos from the East Coast. Born in Ukraine. Overbearing character with murderous instincts. He is madly in love with his younger wife, Krista.

RICO

Bodyguard of Rudy Cuevas, a thug of Colombian origin. Works as a team with Indio Billy.

ROSE (Marvin)

Although, at first, he appears as an unimportant emissary of the Colonel, Agent Rose turns out to be the liaison with a vast federal government agency that intends to use Col. Berkowitz and his former Quadrille "expendable" underlings to carry out their most sordid missions.

WILFRED

The local Quadrille man who serves as Coonan's guide once he lands in Miami following a summons from his former chief.

ZOTOV (Viktor)

A.k.a. Goliath. A former Soviet GRU agent now turned the most feared enforcer of the Russian Mafia in the American continent. Hired by Leo Kaminski as his personal bodyguard.

THE RED ENFORCER

Part One

Prologue

Every effect has its cause, and the one that gave rise to the birth of the Organized Crime Force (also known as the OCF) originated in 1992, during the early days of the fall of Communism in the Soviet Union. Mikhail Yegorov, the first deputy Minister of the Interior of the emerging Russian Federation, traveled to the United States to meet with a certain Arnold Feldman from our State Department, and proposed something that was considered surprising at the time, but which Feldman would later willingly accept, contrary to some of us who actively participated in the Cold War and could never look favorably on the former Bolsheviks. As it turned out, Mr. Yegorov's proposal was based on establishing a bilateral cooperation treaty between the police forces of our two nations, to wage war on the *Organizatsiya* — translated from the Russian as "the Organization" — in a coordinated manner.

In early 1996, with the backing of then Attorney General Jo Ann Woods-Renault and some members of the Senate, who preferred to remain anonymous, the OCF was instituted as a law enforcement agency, second only in government funding to the National Security Agency.

Its authority crossed the oceans and expanded considerably as Washington formalized the treaty with the new and friendly Russian Federation and other rising Eastern European nations.

It was then that, from a guileful State Department official, Arnold Feldman went on to become the "All-American champion" of the coming war against the Russian Mafia. We all understand that most of these high government bureaucrats have a great attachment to political power and deep down they even share the same secret ambition: to gain the presidency of the country one day soon. But what many do not know is that there was a small detachment within the OCF itself, which some legislators ignored at the beginning and whose existence was underwritten by the attorney general. It was a sort of subsection within the mother-agency, a *very* special task force, expendable and dedicated entirely to fighting the most fearsome of the nine Russia Mafia clans operating in the Americas. A vast and very powerful organization, which, at the time, was labeled by the FBI as "an organized criminal cartel equal to, or even more dangerous, than those of Medellin and Cali...."

I am referring to none other than the Ostrovsky Clan.

Despite all the vapid explanations given by the national press, none of us old hands at the Quadrille really understood why the new Potomac gods chose to designate a slick State Department bureaucrat, rather than Col. Marlon Berkowitz, as the chief operating officer of the OCF and handed over complete control of this formidable new security agency to him. For starters, Mr. Feldman had no previous experience in fighting organized crime, nor was he proficient in the clandestine operations field. This man was only a wily diplomat, for God's sake! Nothing else.

But it was not until October 1998 that Arnold Feldman (following the success achieved by the Quadrille in the operation I'm about to recount) was pressured by Attorney General Woods-Renault to appoint the now retired Col. Marlon Berkowitz of the U.S. Special Forces, as the director of operations of this elite succinct unit of handpicked clandestine warriors, which was officially inducted as CI5.

But even to this day, no one knows for sure what the official-sounding acronym means.

There are some who say that this contraction refers to Counterintelligence No. 5, which is only logical because that's exactly what we did, but the only counterintelligence I've ever known about in all my years of undercover service was CI3, a detachment of the FBI that dealt with the illegal spies of the former Soviet KGB operating in Washington, D. C.

Conclusion: already in view of so many significant changes and the arrival of an uncertain new world order, the government of the United States began to prepare for a new kind of war.

Chapter 1

THE MESSENGER

Nassau, Bahamas, in mid-1997.

The hotel is named Atlantis and it had just been inaugurated. It is a palatial mansion built on the emerald waters of the Caribbean Sea, in the heart of a tropical paradise full of that pristine and romantic charm so typical of the Old World. Its architecture is imbued with the same sumptuousness that one tends to find in the spy films featuring Agent 007. Hell, even the gambling house has been christened *Casino Royale*; I guess in honor of Ian Fleming's first novel. If you are curious to know if in those moments I was feeling like "Bond, James Bond," why yes, I suppose I was.

There's nothing wrong with indulging in disposing of a few dollars at the blackjack tables and the slot machines; after all, money is earned to be spent, right? That's the American way of life, a concept that keeps the economy alive and healthy, always thriving and circulating. To hell with the badgering voice of my conscience, I was on leave; or so I thought until I saw the messenger.

At first, I didn't realize he was a courier, of course; we seldom do until they identify themselves as such. This gent was a man of worldly bearing, in his early forties. He was wearing a smart white dinner jacket with a red bow tie, it harmonized with the wide pleated satin sash that ran as a cummerbund over a pair of black pants. His body still looked hard and lean, without the slightest hint of an incipient belly. The truth is that the man looked fit that was probably because he followed a strict daily regime of exercise and a balanced diet. Something that I, if you must know, had ceased working at in those days; so, when you stop to reflect on the events that took place, I must concede that the Colonel acted in a timely manner.

No one like old Marlon Berkowitz to keep his troops from falling into neglect.

Coming back to the messenger, he approached one of the gaming tables and from time to time threw furtive glances in my direction. When I decided to leave my spot and head for the canteen, the man wasted no time in following. He took one of the swivel stools to my right, and it was then that I noticed he was carrying a folded newspaper under his arm. He ordered a Scotch and paid cash to the bartender, adding a tip. Then he turned and walked away, but when the folded newspaper fell to the polished marble floor the man ignored it. I bent down quickly to pick it up and after downing my drink all in one move, I got off the bar stool and headed for my suite.

There's no need to emphasize that I was intensely curious about the melodrama. It had been several years ago, in "92, that the Washington fat cats had opted to disband the Quadrille, our old unit. And now suddenly, just like that, as if by magic, that unexpected man had walked into my life with a return ticket to an uncertain and forgotten world of cloaks and daggers, a world of which little or nothing was left in me.

I mean if that's what this was all about.

Almost eight years had passed since the fall of the Berlin Wall and the collapse of red Russia's Soviet empire.

Between them Mikhail Gorbachev, that gutsy Pole Karol Wojtyla (whom the world also knew as Pope John Paul II), President Ronald Reagan and Margaret Thatcher had given the final boot in the ass to Communism in Europe and the trail of feces left by the Soviets in the Baltic republics was something to watch.

Consequently, these world events had taken me away from the elimination missions which I carried out during the last stage of the Cold War, during the time I served faithfully in the Quadrille under the orders of retired Col. Marlon Berkowitz.

The candid minds on Capitol Hill, as they watched events unfold, decided that keeping a shadow outfit like ours operating in peacetime was not "politically correct." And perhaps they were right about that when one considers our *modus operandi*. The only difference, I think, the *big* difference, between the Commies and us was that ours was a social cleansing unit that instead of focusing on the elimination of enemy personnel abroad, worked hard on preventing all those sons of bitches from messing with us on our own backyard.

After my dismissal in '92, I had survived by killing for hire for a New Orleans broker who served as a contractor for certain Syndicate families, that kept me afloat for about three years. Now I was flying back and forth to South America in a four-seater Cessna. My present endeavor was to deliver weapons and other military supplies to the Castaño brothers, the leaders of a fierce right-wing group called the *Autodefensas Unidas de Colombia* (United Self-Defense Forces of Colombia to you) who had set up camp in the Colombian jungles and were having a blast killing guerrillas of the Revolutionary Armed Forces of Colombia, also known as FARC, in arrangement with some of the local drug lords. Believe it or not, Uncle Sam found their peculiar pastime quite convenient. It was a way to keep the pro-Communist guerrillas at bay without having to send U.S. troops into the region.

Although it may seem so, it was not such a risky job. Almost nothing compared to what I'd done and would do with the Quadrille, under the code name Delta.

Back to my vacation in Nassau, at first, I imagined that the stranger who had approached me in the casino was a messenger sent by my current employer, although I dismissed the thought almost immediately because, in those days, the CIA was in deep water with a Senate commission and my liaisons officer at Langley had ordered me to keep a low profile for a few weeks. Zero trips to Colombia on behalf of The Company; the time had come for me to hang up my guns and indulge in amusement. To compensate for my loss of income due to the cease of operations, I was paid a handsome bonus that also served as a retainer so as not to commit myself in the days to come. The boys from the Planning Department wanted to be sure that they could count on me as soon as the Senate suspended the inquisitions on their activities in the southern cone of the hemisphere.

For a moment I imagined the look of annoyance on the Colonel's face if he were forced to admit to my face that he wanted me back because he *needed* me; certainly a funny notion, because he's a haughty and cantankerous old bastard and it has always been kind of hard for him to openly admit that I was the best of all the "eliminators" he ever had under his command in that world of hushed sentences that always formed part of his life.

Could this be what was really happening, I wondered as I felt the bite of nostalgia.

And suddenly I experienced a wave of déjà vu, recalling all those years of wild youth when my association with the Quadrille allowed me to give free rein to my hunting instincts, the times when I ruled disposing of enemy agents left and right all over the American Union — on rare occasions even abroad — with the purpose of keeping our national security intact.

Had the old fox managed to get back to his old ways? Had he been able to set up his lethal shop again and bring together our old pack?

Hell, I thought, *only one way to find out.*

That same afternoon, once installed in my rented suite at fifteen hundred dollars a night, I leaned against the metal railing of the balcony overlooking the ocean, no shirt on, to enjoy the splendid sea breeze that was blowing up there. I held a glass of ice-cold champagne in my left hand and a Montecristo cigar between my teeth, while the fingers of my right hand clung to the piece of paper I had received with the neatly typed instructions. And yes, truth is that yes, it was a call from him that had been sent to me wrapped in the newspaper delivered to the casino by his messenger. It came with a traveler's checkbook, a U.S. passport with my picture although it had been issued under a false name — Peter S. Barnett, if it matters — and a large amount of cash: mostly dollars and a few hundred million in Colombian pesos.

Great! I thought, *money dropped from the sky... Who will I have to kill this time to earn it?*

Reading the instructions, I recognized the crisp, direct style of his prose.

> **EYES ONLY:**
> Effective immediately you are to cease any activity in which you find yourself engaged at present and take the next available flight to Miami, Florida... We expect

your arrival within the next forty-eight hours... Do not delay, Delta; time is short... Make contact by telephone as soon as you arrive and use your code name.

Judging by the tone of top secret and unquestionable authority he'd employed, combined with the use of my old Quadrille code name, more than a message it could be said to be a direct order — which, of course, it was. He never considered the possibility that I would refuse; for him he was still my boss, and I would obey him until the end of time that was all.

Well, he'd made the rank of colonel in the U.S. Armed Forces for a reason, hadn't he?

The message was not signed, of course; it never is. I read it more than once before burning it with the red tip of my Montecristo and scattered its ashes in the coastal wind, but deep inside me something rebelled against his interference in my private affairs without warning, just like that, and I couldn't stop thinking *why now, dammit, after so long without making contact* and *go fuck yourself, old goat!* at the same time.

"Why now, God dammit!" I shouted angrily at the wind.

Then I came to my senses and figured that if I resented him, he would resent the new gods in the Potomac just as much, after the ingratitude and disregard they'd shown for all of us, disbanding our unit in such abrupt manner, regardless of all the sacrifices we did for God and Country while they needed us.

The difference, I'll say, is that he, Marlon Berkowitz, was always a patriot. And so was I, in the naïve years of my youth; what little was left of that intense feeling that once swelled in my chest was complemented, now in my maturity, by the simple fact that killing for a living is the only thing I have learned to excel in life.

And that's the truth, whether I like it or not.

Chapter 2

THE GUIDE

Going back to colonial times, Miami's early history has always been linked to violence despite the splendorous image of a peaceful and tropical paradise, manufactured for tourism that the city's administrators try so hard to project in their advertising campaigns. After the Civil War, Americans began to contemplate the future in terms of territorial expansion and did not look favorably on the European adventurers who still roamed our continent. In Spain the sale of Florida to the United States was already considered as the only logical course of action, but this idea soon began to lose ground to the appetite of some because pirates turned the Keys and the southern coasts of Florida into a sort of "no man's land," where multiple treacheries were forged, and gangs of murderers dedicated to looting commenced attacking American ships. This convinced Washington that allowing a Spanish Florida was tantamount to giving way to anarchy. In 1811, Yankee troops attacked St. Augustine and ravaged the plantations until they were rejected by British warships. Consequently, the conflagration of 1812 between the United States and Great Britain forced Madrid to allow the latter to take up positions in Florida, something that would add fuel to the fire and further boost the Yankees' anger and our resolve to kick the Europeans out of the far South once and for all. The outcome of the conflict is now history: Florida lost British naval protection and in 1821 Spain surrendered the peninsula to the Americans.

Yet, even today, the Greater Miami government and its well-trained police force have not been able to completely eradicate the epidemic of violence. The Italian Mafia of the 1950s; the CIA conspiracies to overthrow Cuba's Communist tyranny using Cuban exile groups in the 1960s; the hijacking of planes and diversions to Cuba by former Black Panther militants; the assassination operations against exiled leaders and fighters (such as Rolando Masferrer, José Elías de la Torriente and Tony Cuesta, among others) carried out by agents of Communist Cuba in the 1970s; the pitched battles between the Miami Police and DEA agents with Medellin Cartel *sicarios* and the fearsome gangs of *marielitos* who arrived on the Mariel Flotilla in the early 1980s... But more recently, the Russian Mafia operations have helped shape what is today's Miami: a combat zone disguised as a tropical paradise. The same picture painted by pirates centuries ago when Florida was still a Spanish possession.

There are things that never change, no matter who goes or comes, because of the misfortune that some regions have for being in a coveted geographical position that demarcates the channels to growth, wealth, and ultimately political power. Miami — we're all aware of that — also known as the Magic City and the Gateway to the Americas, is the "Sin City" of the Atlantic.

When I landed at Miami International Airport, the Russian Mafia was working its way down from Brighton Beach, N.Y., and in the process of controlling the drug trade and legal gambling in the floating casinos of Fort Lauderdale. At that time, land-based gambling houses were still illegal in the state of Florida, and in Tallahassee the legislature had not yet decided to approve the state lottery concept, although it was already under consideration. The *Organizatsiya* was branching out to the seashores of Hollywood Beach, the Florida Keys, Miami Beach, the million-dollar Bal Harbor zone as well as other more affluent areas of Miami-Dade County, such as the modern luxury condos throughout Brickell Point.

The days of South Beach Art Deco, made fashionable in the *Miami Vice* TV show and Brian de Palma's film *Scarface*, no longer reflected the modus vivendi of undercover cops and bandits out to kill each other. The Floridian Riviera was under construction thanks to the investment in skyscrapers and beach resorts along the Atlantic Coast by billionaires like Donald Trump and other real estate tycoons who bought up almost all the old hotels on Collins Avenue to demolish them and build a new kind of luxury playground for the rich and famous in their place.

I'd been ruminating on all this as I faced the cultural shock triggered by finding such a heterogeneous city that is in no way representative of the rest of the Union — at least, in its purest essence. In Miami, English has become the "second language" of its inhabitants, sometimes even the "third" in certain areas of the Northeast side where a large colony of Haitian refugees has settled. But the fact is that Spanish predominates in almost every area of Miami-Dade County. In addition, signs in Spanish, English, and Creole chase you all over the international airports, reminding the Latin American tourists that *Aquí se sentirán como en su casa*, or, in other words: "Feel right at home!"

I left the huge, refrigerated terminal only to find myself in the heat, which the strong South Florida sun and high humidity make a sticky and uncomfortable condition in the hours around noon. I immediately looked for a phone booth, and found one, which I used to place the call to the number I'd memorized back in Nassau.

"Yes?" an unfamiliar voice answered.

"The code is Delta, I just arrived. I'm standing outside the Caribbean Airlines terminal and await instructions."

"How was your trip, Delta?"

"Uneventful. Nothing to report."

"Any problems at Customs?"

"None; as I said, everything's fine."

"Well, look around, you will see a cab with the number 28 painted on the tail... Do you spot it?"

"Affirmative, one from the Sunny Cab fleet," I said after scanning the taxi's pickup stand with my eyes and locating the indicated vehicle.

"That's correct. Get on board; the driver's name is Wilfred, local talent. He'll bring you to the safehouse."

"Understood."

I returned the handset to the hanger and stepped out

of the cab. Outside, I motioned for Wilfred to pick me up. I reached into my flight bag feeling naked with no weapons on me and marveled at how quickly the training returns to your senses once the brain digests that you're back in the saddle and every new character you meet becomes a potential foe. That's what the cloak and dagger frat boys instill in you from the moment you get initiated in the trade. Our motto is: *Trust no one.*

I took out a pair of sunglasses from my handbag and put them on; retinal relief from the harsh Miami sunrays sank in immediately.

Judging by his physical appearance, Wilfred must've been in his thirties; possibly the first half. He was a dark-haired, suntanned Cuban-American with a sinewy build and a deceptively affable expression on his face; he had green cat-like eyes that kept watching everything around him as he drove, but they did so in the same systematic, analytical and underhanded way I had noticed before in the clandestine warriors of the CIA, on the one hand, and the undercover agents of the DEA, on the other. Not to mention the FBI sleuths.

Of course, the sharpness of his gestures was better perceived in him because his Caribbean idiosyncrasy did not allow him to spend much time unnoticed; the natives of the Antilles islands — and I mean any of them — love to draw attention to themselves. He had probably heard of me, and the man wanted to be sure I treated him as an equal, not a rookie, and the only way he could prove his worth to me for the time being was to make his mental acuity obvious. I, on the other hand, prefer others to think of me as mediocre until it's time to turn the tables on them. What can I say, it's a matter of style.

The first thing Wilfred did, something I approved of, was to give me a tour of the area called Little Havana. My tacit acceptance was not so much in response to a deep cultural interest, although I was seduced by the possibility of seeing the famous Domino Park that always appears in the photos of the tourist brochures when they show you the attractions of the folkloric 8th Street. We toured several typical Cuban bars and restaurants, including the Miami version of *La bodeguita del medio*, in Miracle Mile, and a restaurant named *La esquina de Tejas*, which became nationally famous the year President Reagan traveled to Miami to have lunch there in the company of the Cuban exile community leaders who supported his political campaigns. This was the capital of West Indian anti-Communism, where many conspiracies had germinated to overthrow a fierce tyranny.

Wilfred took me on a passing tour of a site located at an intersection on Ponciana Boulevard, between Le Jeune and Douglas Road, where he explained that a very special house once stood on that corner, sheltered by trees that concealed a dense garden and a very tall fence. The house had been rented by a certain E. Howard Hunt — if the name sounds familiar it's because it belonged to an American spy thriller novelist who was also a CIA agent, and who had conspired with the Cuban fighter Manuel Artime and his group of *brigadistas* to overthrow Fidel — and who, after the frustrated landing at the Bay of Pigs, would spend more than two years in prison for his involvement in the Watergate Hotel scandal, during Richard Nixon's presidency.

Anyway, I found it fascinating to know the historical

background of all this, but I was even more pleased to see that this Wilfred character was a first-class driver and that our tours of the so-called Magic City served to prove that we had not yet attracted any unwanted attention. That is to say: We had no tail — not yet anyway.

Finally, after visiting the smoke shops on 8th Street, having a couple of *fritas* and a *batido de mamey* at *La esquina de Tejas*, finishing off lunch with a cup of Cuban coffee (something I did in memory of old Reagan) and stocking up on a few Montecristo cigars, we headed north on Le Jeune Road and crossed Northwest 36th Street, which at the height of Le Jeune can be considered the border between Miami and Hialeah. But soon I could see that The City of Progress was not going to be our destination, the safehouse had been set up even further north, in an old, abandoned warehouse of an industrial park, where the Colonel had established his new workshop. As soon as I saw the layout, I understood his reasons for choosing such a ramshackle site, which was not only in a plebeian zone, devoid of folkloric color, but also located very close to the Miami-Opa Locka Executive Airport. For a shadow network like the Quadrille, it was vitally important to have its head-quarters near a private airstrip — and a paramilitary one at that.

*C*hapter *3*

THE OPA LOCKA SAFEHOUSE

On our way to the city of Opa Locka we left behind the world-famous Hialeah Park, another icon of the days when *Miami Vice* made all of us who watched the show believe that the city of Miami was full of pink flamingos and all that exotic fauna that finds its habitat in the grounds of the Conservatory, an annex to the racetrack. I would have liked to have a peek at them, of course, and perhaps witness one or two of the horse races announced for the season; but that did not happen.

When I told Wilfred so, the guide smiled and said: "Everyone thinks those pink flamingos are native to these parts. Not so, man, they were imported from Cuba in 1930 by the National Audubon Society. Did you know that?"

"Nope," I said, "not really. I thought they were part of the local fauna."

"Well, they are now; but you're not going to find them anywhere else outside the Conservatory."

Wilfred went on driving up East Fourth Avenue after articulating two or three more explanatory phrases intended to enrich my meager knowledge of the area and continued to chauffeur the cab with fluid skill until he reached the street bordering the southern edge of Amelia Earhart Park. Pretending to pay attention to what the man was saying, I discreetly checked the mirrors again; still, no one tailing us. In a few more minutes we arrived at our destination.

The guide parked about twenty meters away from the warehouse entrance.

"Get out and walk up to the gate, I will wait for you here."

"Okay," I said, grabbed my flight bag, and walked to where I was pointed to. I could have left the suitcase in the car, but the idea did not appeal to me. One does not survive in this business by trusting everyone who is introduced to you as an ally, even if they really are.

When I reached the main doors of the premises, I noticed that they were being watched by closed circuit cameras, conveniently camouflaged in the facade and both flanks of the building, although not well enough to deceive a trained eye like mine. The entrance was guarded from the inside. This was confirmed by the fact that I didn't even have to knock on the doors upon arrival, they were opened from the inside with a metallic click preceded by a faint electronic buzz. I entered and suddenly found myself engulfed in a sea of gloom; it was as if my life had suddenly been painted black.

"Easy, Delta," hissed the same voice I'd heard on the phone upon arrival, "just let yourself go. I'll lead the way."

"Okay," I said.

A large, rough man's hand took me by one elbow and began to guide me. I let him do it, of course. Gradually, as we walked along, the room began to dimly light up until we came to a backlit silhouetted door at whose lintel we stopped before my contact pushed it open.

"Go in, *amigo*," he said, "Col. Berkowitz is waiting for you."

To see him again, after all the time that had elapsed, was not as shocking as I had expected: He was just the same as I had left him when we said goodbye one autumn afternoon in his Washington office, on the banks of the Anacostia River, where the walls and all the decorations were as plain, gray and antiseptic as his own spirit. The Gray Specter, he was called by some members of the Senate Select Committee on Intelligence Matters, partly because of his preference for that morbid color and because he'd mastered to perfection the poker face technique of not showing his emotions under any circumstances, but it was a skill he began to lose along with patience as the years went by, when life began to hit him hard and often. However, when it came to clandestine operations, Colonel Marlon Berkowitz was a real iceberg, capable of burning your soul with the mere intensity of his frosted gaze.

"You've let yourself grow fat," was the first thing he said, by way of greeting, "I'm not sure that's convenient for this operation, perhaps it is, because you don't look one bit like a government agent. Besides, you've grown sideburns, and your hair is not as neatly trimmed as I remember you... What have you been doing with your life all this time, Delta? You look more like a greasy, unkempt Third World mercenary than that young elite soldier, as sharp and pointy as a stiletto that I once recruited... Well, what else can you expect these days when guerrillas and paramilitarism have become so fashionable. Mm?"

He was sitting behind a desk, as usual, and there was no one else but us in that room; that is, there didn't *seem* to be, but I was soon to find out that this was not the case.

"Thank you, Colonel. You're still as neat and tidy as ever, the same son of a bitch who disposed of the stiletto in the trash bin when it was no longer useful as a tool... What have you been doing with your life all this time? Mm?"

Resentment surfaced in my words, although I thought I had prepared myself well for this moment to behave with the same equanimity he'd instilled in all of us to handle adverse situations. But then I realized that, deep down, I still had it in for him, or the boys from Capitol Hill for that matter, and Marlon Berkowitz understood it.

"Good Heavens, I see that you have deteriorated far more than I imagined; now, besides a foul-mouthed creature, you have also become a disrespectful one," he said lowering his voice and hardening it. "Maybe it was a mistake to send for you...."

His voice trailed off, generating suspense, and, in a seemingly casual movement, his right hand began to open one of the top desk drawers. I couldn't help myself, before the Colonel could complete the move, I dropped my suitcase on the floor and flew over the desk like a missile fired at him. The fingers of his right hand gripped the butt of the Colt .38 he kept in the drawer, when mine clamped around his throat.

The office was flooded with people at that instant and before I could crush his windpipe, four powerful arms pinned me down and separated me from him. Then I felt the impact of a karate chop on the back of my neck and my lights went out.

I regained consciousness surprised to find myself alive; the Colonel was still occupying the swivel chair behind his desk, and I'd been stuffed into an armchair that someone had placed in front of his escritoire. The office was again occupied only by the two of us.

"Calm down, Delta," he spoke in a soothing voice, "it was just a test which, in fact, you passed admirably well even though you look like a walking disaster. I'm glad to see, for the umpteenth time in my already long life, that appearances can be deceiving."

He said this with a mischievous grin on his lips.

Without a word, I quickly scanned the room to locate the revolver and found it resting on top of his desk with the business end of the firearm not pointing in my direction.

My reaction didn't pass unnoticed.

"Take it easy, will you? The gun is not loaded. It was just a test of your reflexes."

"Yes, sir. I'm sorry."

"Me too; I'll admit it was not the ideal way to greet the best and most loyal of the men under my command, but you understand that this is a tough business, Delta, and tough you *really* must be to survive in it."

Now he really had me baffled... Had I heard correctly? Had he admitted what I thought I'd heard from his tight mouth? *To the best and most faithful of the men under my command...*

Unbelievable! Did the old fox need me that much?

"Well, uh, thank you, sir," I mumbled with calculated humility. "Just doing my duty."

"And you did it quite well indeed, eh," he said widening his smile before turning serious again, "but hostilities and praise aside, I'll cut to the chase because time is pressing. There is a possibility that we can go back to being what we were. Would you be interested in coming back to work for us?"

He always allowed me to choose or made me believe that I was permitted to do so in my decisions. Ah, beautiful democracy.

"Of course, sir. I don't know how to do anything else."

He gave me a terse smirk again.

"Splendid," he said quickly, "you will use the money I sent you with the courier to pay your way out of your previous arrangement with the CIA. If it's not enough, just let me know, but I want that contract dissolved *now*. Return that last bonus they gave you to the boys at Langley, you copy? As you've probably guessed, it was meant as a retainer."

"Yes, sir," was my automatic response while my brain registered that he'd been keeping an eye on me all this time and was aware of my dealings with the Company.

"That should square you with them, if they give you trouble, let me know and I'll take it up from there. Any way you look at it, the boys in the Planning Department are toast, the Senate Select Committee on Intelligence Matters have them under the magnifying glass."

I would not have been surprised at all if he'd been the one pulling the strings behind the scenes so that the CIA's relationship with the Colombian AUC would fall apart and free me of my commitment to the Company.

It was now obvious that he wanted me, once again, under his iron fist. I rubbed the back of my neck where I'd been hit and noticed the spot was swelling.

"Are they really going to reactivate us?" I asked.

"There is a possibility it will happen, yes, but there are no guarantees so far."

"Are the Russians back to their old ways, sir?"

"In a way they are, although not at government level. I understand that they're making amendments to change their system and turn the country into a representative democracy, Boris Yeltsin has good intentions, but the problem we face today is not directly with the new Russian Federation, but with the former members of the KGB and the military hardliners."

"The same bullies who tried to give Gorbachev the coup d'état," I said.

"Exactly. It seems they have convinced themselves that a return to the days of Soviet tyranny is not feasible for now and have started to leave the country, don't you know. They are fleeing Moscow *en masse*, Delta, as rats do when the ship is sinking, to close ranks with the *Organizatsiya*."

And that was the very first time I ever heard of the Russian Mafia.

*C*hapter *4*

THE PLAYERS

Strangely enough, I felt suddenly ashamed for allowing myself to have gained all the excess weight I was carrying around and for neglecting my aesthetic appearance. That's what I experienced as soon as my brain accepted that "the wolf had returned to the pack" and it was time to sharpen all fangs and claws to go out hunting again; because hunting is best done when the beast is "lean and hungry," not as "fat and satiated" as I'd become working for Langley.

"Is something wrong, Delta? You seem distracted," said my boss, pausing to glare at me.

I drew a long breath. "I, uh... I'm sorry, sir. I've just realized how wrong I've been to neglect my form... I should never have...."

He grinned. "May I tell you something? It was a *blessing* that you did. The task I have for you will be easier to accomplish with that new look you have," he said winking an eye, "than if you were in the same elite soldier form you were in when we parted ways."

"Are you serious, Colonel?"

"But of course. Now you'll see why...."

He paused to pull out his briarwood pipe, fill the stinging bowl with apple-scented tobacco and then light it.

"You may smoke," he said. "Would you like a coffee, or something stronger?"

"Coffee is fine, sir, black and no sugar. Thank you."

Another terse smile and he lifted the intercom handset he had on the bureau to give the order.

While someone in another section of the safehouse was getting the coffee ready for us, the Colonel devoted a few minutes to gather his thoughts while he smoked and, I suppose, allow time for the coffee to be brought to us.

The man who entered the room a short time later, carrying a plastic tray with a thermal carafe on top and two white porcelain cups, was the same individual who had contacted me in Nassau, and when he spoke, I recognized the voice that had answered the phone when I'd called from the airport upon arrival. It was the same deep voice that had greeted me in the darkness at the entrance to the shelter and had guided me in the dark to the Colonel's office.

"This is Marvin, Delta. We are counting on his assistance in this matter. Marvin does not belong to the Quadrille, but he is with a sister-agency, you don't need to know which, with interests in the case at hand that are none of your business either...."

Marvin smirked, but refrained from looking at me as he did so, so as not to rub salt in the wound. His gesture was not lost on me, and I sort of accepted it, but then my eyes noticed that the edge of his right hand was slightly swollen and reddened; that changed everything... He had been the bugger who had knocked me out with a karate chop to the back of the head. I've never looked kindly on those who hit me, or shoot me, whoever they are and regardless of motive. From that moment on I marked him for retribution.

Great! I thought with sarcasm, because I hate those last-minute details that are "none of my business," as it almost always turns out that, had I learned about them beforehand, my task would have been easier. But, where the captain is the master, the sailor is not, so I had no choice but to take a deep breath and adapt to the situation.

I noticed that the one called Marvin didn't need a seat. He squared himself before the Colonel's desk, with his hands clasped behind his back and his legs apart to keep his balance... It was the typical stance of those who practice martial arts, always seeking harmony and stability of the body.

"Marvin," my boss asked softly, "would you be so kind as to bring Buchinsky's file and the Kaminskis', please?

Marvin hesitated for a moment and then it was my turn to grin at him with jovial malice, but his hesitation lasted only a second; ipso facto he nodded his head, articulated a spur-of-the-moment "yes, sir" and left the room. He was not amused that the Colonel used him not only as a messenger and contact person, but now also as a servant. That's called getting "triple-mileage" out of the agents, and it's considered unethical by the current protocol of a federal agency, but since the Quadrille never existed — a least, officially — my boss was always an expert at ignoring that rule.

Anyway, it turned out that Dave Buchinsky, despite bearing a surname of Lithuanian origin, was an American, born in Brighton Beach, New York, to Lithuanian parents. To the Russian Mafia rooted in Brighton Beach, Buchinsky was what the boys from Brooklyn and Topeka call a "mechanic," a hitman. The Russians — the Colonel later explained to me — also had a name for it: *boyevik*. But in any language or dialect, Big Dave was a gunman for hire, a private enforcer who didn't work for any one gang exclusively because he was considered sort of a specialist and sold his deadly skills to the highest bidder. In the grapevine of all organized crime on the East Coast, Buchinsky had a reputation as a quick and lethal shooter. His weapon of choice was an admirably old but well-preserved World War II Walther P-38 semi-auto, which he loaded with 9mm Parabellum "dum-dum" bullets — the kind that explode on impact. In Brighton Beach he was known by a sobriquet: The Butcher. The moniker fit him well because, according to his file, the man was considered one of the worst blood-thirsty gangsters by the FBI, whose agents had him ranked in the same league as Bonnie and Clyde. He was said to kill devilishly well and enjoyed doing it.

On the other hand, Leonid Kaminski had managed to emigrate to America before the Iron Curtain came down. He had done so at the beginning of the 1980s, as part of a large emigration of Slavic Jews that had been arranged by both superpowers during a round of negotiations in which the U.S. was asking for signs of political aperture from the USSR in exchange for American wheat price rebates. Leo Kaminski, who initially settled in St. Petersburg, Florida, came from Ukraine and after a couple of years decided to move to Brighton Beach, where he met and married his blonde wife, Krista. It was there that he entered the underworld of organized crime.

That was the information contained in the file.

"These bastards," spoke Marvin, referring to the couple, "are on a roll. Their upward trajectory in the Brighton Beach underworld is to be admired for the promptness in which they have carved out their own niche on the East Coast. And now they're in the process of expanding their business... these, uh, Ukrainians are savages straight out of the Middle Ages. This man is as despicable as he is brutal; so are the *boyeviks* under his command. Even the Russians fear them..., they love to work with axes and machetes: they cut off ears, fingers, noses, and genitals. But you better watch out, they gouge out eyes too!"

"Well, if it's like that, they are behind the times," I said, grinning wolfishly, "the Colombians use electric saws, for God's sake!"

The Colonel stared at me grimly, as if he were trying to shut me up, before he turned to the other man and ordered him: "Marvin, please, go get the slide projector, will you?"

Marvin blushed and struggled not to lose his temper, but when he was able to control himself, he only mumbled a sparse "yes, sir" and left the office to carry out the order.

"I feel sorry for him," the Colonel spoke, looking at me with a trace of shame in his eyes, "he's not a bad fellow, but I'm unconsciously taking out on him all the contempt his chief inspires in me...."

"May I know who he is?" I asked.

"His boss? A man you'd rather not get close to. In some way I don't understand, he's managed to get himself into some very high places in the Washington political arena. But make no mistake, Delta, the man is a hyena."

"Really? Well, Washington is a very shifting arena these days, sir," I spat. "By the way, who is this man, exactly?"

"His name is Arnold Feldman, and he comes from the State Department, but I don't think you know him or have heard of him; he moves in very different circles from us."

"He's not connected to the CIA?"

"Not at all. At least, as far as I know... But, if you don't object, I'd rather get back to the subject of your mission.

"As you wish, sir."

Actually, I would have liked to delve more into that insidious situation, but with the Old Man it was better not to press. If at some point he decided to come clean with me and tell me about his tribulations with this Feldman character, he would do so; in the meantime, it was best not to show undue interest.

Just then Marvin returned with the image projector and a box full of slides. At that time computers were not yet as accessible as they are today, and I remind you that the Quadrille was not even in operation, although we were in the process of getting back into the swing of things.

For the next hour, the torrent of images that scrolled across the screen gave me a vivid overview of all the players I would be cavorting against in this match. Of all the pictures I viewed, the ones that struck me the most were those of Krista Kaminski... *Wow, what a woman!* She looked like a Valkyrie, those blonde Amazons of Viking lineage that always made my Nordic fantasies fly high — when I had them. From the moment I laid eyes on her, I longed for her body.

The plot that Marvin and my boss laid out for me was quite interesting, even though it deviated from the basis on which I had been trained as a professional assassin in the secret service of my country's interest, even though I'm not officially tagged as that. Washington is famous for using euphemisms, and I was always labelled an "eliminator," an eliminator of problems. Whether the eliminations were conducted with firearms, edged weapons or explosives was totally irrelevant to the national security chieftains, of course. But the motives behind my actions, up to the present, have always been political and/or military. What these two were presenting to me now was a different kettle of fish; it fell into the category of law enforcement because it involved (at least at first glance) drug trafficking and gambling.

"We know Leo Kaminski as The Sower," said Marvin.

"The Sower?" I asked.

"Well, he owns a marijuana plantation near Lake Okeechobee," clarified my boss, "among other things."

"And now he plans to establish a line of floating casinos in the Florida Keys," Marvin said. "He has become an entrepreneur with vision."

"Ambitious guy, isn't he?"

"Yes... It seems so, but it's his wife who motivates him and constantly demands more from him; he is crazy about her and as he needs more and more money to keep her happy, so he must keep exploring new markets."

"I don't blame him," I commented sardonically, earning the frowning attention of both men. "A woman like that is worth enjoying every single day, what curves for God's sake... Whew!"

The Colonel smiled sharply while Marvin glared at me, and I put on a beatific expression on my face to spur him on even more. But the Old Man surprised me when his features suddenly lit up, and he pointed his right index finger at me:

"Oh, bless your silly remarks, Delta, you just gave me a great idea!"

Chapter 5

TO THE SEWERS

My boss's "great idea" (which, in his own words, he'd gotten from my "silly remarks"), meant for me a little over a year of my life inside Leo Kaminski's gang, playing badass gangster among those cavemen from the old Ukraine. A gang that even the new militia forces of the Russian Federation feared like kids fear ogres hiding in the closet. Because monsters they were, mind you; let's be clear on that. To survive a year among them I was compelled to become one more of these abominable creatures.

It was also a new experience for me. My service to the country had been first as an active military man and then as a very special secret agent, chosen and trained exclusively to perform a certain kind of work, which not all of us (even those who are part of the elite corps) are mentally capable of doing.

Anyway, here's the story:

Coming down from Brighton Beach, Leo Kaminski had bought land in a rural central Florida allotment near Lake Okeechobee. He had built a huge ranch there, which he called Double K, and had dedicated himself to growing marijuana. He did very well, and with the proceeds he went on the hunt for another, more ambitious prospect which, at least until gambling was legalized on Florida soil — which was bound to happen anyway, though many were unaware of it — was tantamount to having his own gold mine.

Oh, he soon made enemies, *many* enemies, especially in Colombia, where he had tried to explore new routes in Santiago de Cali, the so-called kingdom of rum and sugar cane, salsa and Pachanga (but also of vice, of course) where the extradition of the Rodríguez Orejuela brothers to the United States had left a void that many landsharks were bidding for, although few could fill it because of the sustained pressure that our DEA continued to exert. In Cali he also met a certain Rudy Cuevas, a well-connected local crook who claimed to be his "invisible partner" in the floating casinos operation.

Although Marvin and his boss didn't know it, the Colonel's objective at the time was not to dismantle the Kaminski gang or to lay our hands on The Butcher; although to infiltrate the former I was obliged to get rid of the latter and usurp his place. To do so, I had to spend a few weeks studying him well before making a move on him: Was he left or right-handed? What brand of cigarettes did he smoke? What type of hookers did he prefer? What bars did he visit, and which hotels did he patronize? Favorite restaurants, cinemas, gyms, barbershops, nightclubs, gambling houses; in short, everything I could find out about him. The only thing I didn't try, for lack of time, was to access his medical records and study them at leisure. But, of everything I learned about him, the most useful detail was that the man had a crippled wrist: the left one.

That was his Achilles heel.

I ambushed him in a New Orleans saloon on his way down to Florida to meet The Sower, who was offering him a tidy sum to protect his operation and his wife while he went to seek his fortune in Colombia. To protect himself in Santiago de Cali, Kaminski hired the services of another professional thug of international stature. Cuevas had offered to lend him two of his deadliest boys, a couple of first-class toughies named Rico and Indio Billy, but Kaminski turned them down for The Butcher and Goliath.

I was always curious to learn what was so extra-ordinary about The Butcher that earned him that exaggerated reputation. He lasted me less than a cream pie at the school gate at dismissal time. I disposed of him coming out of a Bourbon Street saloon; it was a clean and simple job: a stab to the heart, which he didn't see coming, before slitting his throat and beheading him afterwards. A gory job, I know, but the orders were to make it look like one of those grotesque Mafia executions in *The Godfather* movie fashion. I was also forced to cut off his hands and dissolve them later in a tankette with acid, along with his cut off head, to make it difficult for anyone to recognize the corpse. Those were the instructions Col. Berkowitz gave me, and it was while executing his orders that I fully understood why he'd admitted to my face that I was the "best and most loyal of the men under his command...."

The old fox was right, there wasn't another man in the world that I would take an order like that from, because what I had to do in that operation didn't take a Ranger Corps sniper turned clandestine operative; that little job took a lot more: It took a bloody psychopath!

Presently I understood why that faceless government agency, to which Marvin was attached, had brought Colonel Berkowitz and his bad boys into the game. It was a sordid job that no one wanted because you had to descend to the sewers and get your hands dirty with excrement.

Chapter 6

FOOL'S ERRAND

Looking at me sideways, Krista Kaminski said:

"I will make you a deal, Dave, I'll give you twenty-five thousand dollars and my body as often as you like for a whole week; you can do with it whatever you desire."

This happened several months later, when, posing as David Buchinsky, I'd become head of security in charge of the men Leo Kaminski had guarding his wife in the Florida Keys, from where he planned to operate his fleet of floating casinos.

"Do what with whom?" I asked, pretending not to understand her.

"With my body, asshole!" she hissed, obviously aggravated by my reaction. "This is your golden opportunity, the one you've always longed for... Don't think I haven't noticed that you can't take your eyes off my ass."

I won't deny it, her rear end was worthy of a monument in Mallory Square. Her bust too.

"Don't play games with me, Krista," I warned her, "I might take you at your word. Your old man is not here to stop me."

She smiled deviously and looked into my eyes in a strange way, which I couldn't interpret at the time. It seemed like a knowing look, but simultaneously tinged with doubts about an implicit complicity.

"You can go for it; I'm serious, Dave. You've always wanted to have me, haven't you? Well, this is your chance, big man. My *ass* is yours! Do you accept?"

I drew a long breath. "Okay..." I said, "who do I have to kill?"

But, of course, that was a silly question; we both knew very well who it was without mentioning it out loud.

Holding my gaze, her mouth articulated the name without any sounds.

I tried to tell her she could go to hell, but I was unable to utter one single word once her unexpected offer had set my fantasies flying. Those "Nordic fantasies" I mentioned earlier.

Then I realized what kind of trouble I was getting into, and I felt anger. I had the uneasy feeling that, somehow, this blonde mare of a bitch was setting me up for her husband; Kaminski would rip my balls off if he ever found out I'd toyed with her. On multiple occasions I had endured those tasteless scenes in which Leo Kaminski forced me to watch him cut off the genitals, fingers, ears, and noses of those who displeased him. The man was an expert at wielding a set of small but heavy and very sharp axes with which he claimed the respect of his troops and spread panic among his enemies.

"All right, Krista." I suddenly agreed, almost not quite believing what I was doing, "I accept!"

That was the instant when my brain suddenly assimilated that the time had come to shed the Dave Buchinsky personality and assume, with all its consequences, my real identity.

Becoming Patrick Coonan, or Agent Delta, was quite a mission. Seeing the arrogant Krista so sure of herself made me lose my temper. I couldn't control myself and hit the coffee table hard with my fist. She made no comment, and I hated her even more for her silence. The problem was that I desired her as body as badly as I wanted to slap her face. That's what I wanted, really, to slap her face and make her swallow all her hurtful phrases and that overconfidence she showed in being able to manipulate me at her will. She was just like her husband. They were just as savage and just as vicious! Neither of them deserved my empathy.

I ran my eyes over her luscious body — slowly this time — and became aroused. Krista noticed it immediately for she was a worldly woman and well acquainted with the lower passions that nestle in the basement of every man's heart. She parted her lips and moistened them with the tip of her tongue.

"Come here, buster, come on..." she hissed, "give it to me, now!"

I stripped off the P-38 that had once made history with its rightful owner and left it on the table in its armpit holster. Krista took off her blouse and miniskirt and walked in her heels to the sliding panel overlooking the balcony, stopping right in front of it. Thank goodness our room was on one of the higher floors of the hotel in which we were staying. Otherwise, her incredible breasts pressed hard against the glass sliding panels, would have caused pile-up in Mallory Square.

"Come on, naughty boy, don't keep me waiting!" She urged me on and hit the glass with the palms of both hands, but not hard enough to break it. That, naturally, was all part of the show.

Krista tilted her golden head to one side and the lush tawny mane spilled over her shoulders, falling down her back with mellifluous languor.

"Jesus..." I grunted under my breath and advanced

towards her.

I got to her side, bucking like a fighting bull, and freed her from the tight black lingerie that made her look so maddeningly desirable. To top off her cheap act of erotic theatre, she shoved her hindquarters against my body and rubbed on my lower abdomen in a sensual gesture. Her pale face — now showing a sly smile — turned to stare at me with a gleam of mockery and defiance in her eyes.

I was unable to delay my part in her act any longer, I set both my hands on her delicious hips, and did what was expected of me....

Later, as I sat smoking on the balcony and sipped a double whisky, I reflected that Krista's plan to leave her husband — if she was sincere — was relatively simple: Get rid of the bodyguards who had accompanied us on this short visit to the Florida Keys and vanish. Meanwhile, the husband was still in Colombia making contacts.

We had time to talk it over after she allowed me to enjoy her body at my leisure in that hotel room. I think I even experienced a certain unhealthy pleasure in screwing her in such a violent way, without an atom of tenderness, as if she were a cheap whore to whom you could do anything.

"What now?" I asked once I had caught my breath.

"You've had your fill, haven't you?" she asked by way of reply.

I said I had.

"Well," she went on as she slipped back into the tight clothes she'd removed to give me pleasure, "start by killing those two jerks in the next room," she said and pointed with a careful index finger towards the adjoining chamber, from which only a door separated us.

Her command puzzled me; among "those two jerks" — as she so contemptuously put it — was the man I knew to be her lover, the one with whom she fornicated most, a strapping lad named Aleksei with the looks of an Olympic gymnast. That made me realize that the darned Krista didn't care for anyone.

Playing the submissive lover, I nodded my head and grabbed for the leather strap carrying the armpit holster and the Walther P-38 I'd taken off to screw my Nordic princess. I tightened up the fastening around my plexus, pulled out the German pistol and checked the clip: eight rounds with a full load. I pulled back the slide of the gun and the first cartridge in line slipped into the chamber with an oily click; then there was the dry metallic sound of the slide moving forward to cover the barrel.

Krista watched me with an expression of malevolent interest.

"Will you do it for me, hon?" she gasped, getting excited.

I drew a long breath.

"You just wait and see...."

I took a determined step towards the door that separated us from the other room where the bodyguards were resting. I opened it with a jerk and the first to realize something was wrong was Karl the redhead, who stared at me in awe and tried to draw his weapon but could not... No one can with a 9mm slug lodged between the eyes.

Aleksei went for his weapon, but I beat him to it. I didn't hit him squarely with my first shot, which only grazed his neck, but the second one split his windpipe.

"Now I want to collect, bitch!" I yelled at Krista as I returned to our room, "Where are those bloody twenty-five grand?

Gathering from the tone in which I addressed her, she began to suspect that the situation was getting out of control.

"Hey, calm down, will you? I'm going to call someone to bring the dough, okay?" she said in a tremulous voice.

I walked up to her and hit her with a couple of slaps that resounded like gunshots.

"You, brute!" she shrieked and tried to slink away, but I grabbed her by the hair, forced her to tilt her face and slapped her again.

If you must know, I don't find any pleasure in slapping women around, but this was a job I had to do, and I was impersonating a very tough customer, a killer extraordinaire from the East Coast underworld, Dave Buchinsky, a man who wasn't supposed to have any qualms about hitting *anybody*, male or female....

In any case, the time had come to turn the table on these people.

The following night the husband came to rescue her, although he made it clear that the exchange — for the ransom money I'd demanded for his wife — was to take place at his ranch in Clewiston, not in Key West. It was obvious that the bastard really loved her, because despite knowing that he was at the top of the FBI's Most Wanted list, he paid no mind to the fact and showed up in Florida with a million bucks in cash.

By the time the great Kaminski arrived in Clewiston, I was tired of banging his wife; and so was she, for that matter. But in the long run, the blonde she-devil got me good. Not only did her husband rush to her rescue with the money I'd demanded in exchange for his luscious lady, but he also brought with him the most dangerous of all the thugs on his payroll. The burly gunman they called Red Goliath.

This made me feel clever, in a way, because neither of them suspected at the time that I was counting on him doing just that. Well, that's what I thought.

When I brought the car to a halt at a bend in the dusty Zambria Street, just before entering the grounds of the Double K Ranch, it was already close to midnight. I looked at Krista with satisfaction before pulling her out of the vehicle. She was unrecognizable with her blonde hair now dyed black — a process I had subjected her to change her appearance somewhat, thus throwing off any of Kaminski's men who might be searching the streets for us — and wearing such baggy clothes that hid all her curves. Her face was haggard and devoid of make-up; her lips were pale, without the seductive effect of the expensive lip crayons she liked so much; her eyes were irritated from crying hard. More than the beautiful wife of a prosperous drug dealer, she looked like a drug addict. Krista must have thought I was going to kill her and leave her corpse lying among the brush, because I had to poke her in the ribs with the Walther's silencer to get her to finally leave the SUV. I felt a little pity for her, because of the disheveled way she looked now, and had to force myself to bare my teeth in a ferocious grin and threaten her that if she did not get out of the car by her own doing, I would get her to do it the hard way.

She went out.

I followed.

She got to walk a few uncertain steps when my harsh command to halt stopped her dead in her tracks.

"Turn around now, Krista." I said softly.

She didn't want to; she couldn't bear to face the inevitable.

"Turn around, or I'll drop you right here!" I hissed.

She turned around shaking and whimpering uncontrollably. When we were face to face, I raised the handgun and aimed the barrel at the center of her forehead.

She closed her eyes.

I drew a long breath and cocked the hammer.

It was too bad I'd been ordered not to leave any lose ends.

*C*hapter 7

DEATH HAS ARRIVED

The time I spent with the Kaminski gang, working undercover, made me aware of some crucial data that came in handy when the moment of truth arrived. One of them was knowing the exact location of that two-and-a-half-acre ranch the Ukrainian mobster owned near Lake Okeechobee. His property was not exactly in Clewiston, you arrive at it right before reaching that town; it lay within the boundaries of a private estate called Montura Ranch Estates. The Double K ranch was located almost at the end of the secluded Zambria Street. As a property it wasn't worth much, trust me, because we're talking about a remote rural area, although it's perfect for raising and keeping horses, cattle, and any kind of domestic animals you can think of. But this suited the great Kaminski just fine, because his ranch was the perfect place for keeping a vast marijuana plantation.

The satellite photos to which I had access through the Internet showed that the Double K ranch was at the back. And to give you an idea of how remote his place was — something extremely convenient for what I had in mind — imagine that that community had been designed with streets and avenues that followed each other in alphabetical order, that is, those named Avenida del Club (starting in A), Camino Real (C), Horse Club Avenue (H), Jinete Road (J), etcetera, etcetera, were located much closer to the clubhouse — the most central and coveted section of the entire development, from the smart buyer's point of view — than a street whose name began in Z.

Get the picture?

It was the perfect place for the grand Kaminski to plant and grow his marijuana undetected, and of which I was going to take advantage to carry out the exchange of an outraged but still healthy wife for a beautiful one million greenbacks stamped with the American dollar sign. If you stop to think about it, the isolation of the terrain suited him too, I suppose, because being familiar with his way of thinking, I dare assure you that Mr. Leo Kaminski never considered the possibility that, after what I'd done to his wife, he will leave me in a position to walk out of the Double K Ranch on my own two feet. The man would chop them off with his hatchet set. But the mobster never guessed I had no intention of walking out on him. As I've said before, I'd been planning to meet him there for other purposes....

The dossier we kept on Goliath said that the Russian agent had schooling — military schooling, that is. But this was nothing new, most of the enforcers who kill for the Russian Mafia have a military background; almost all of them either belonged to the former KGB or spent time with the Red Army fighting in Afghanistan. But this oversized son of a bitch had been a member of the Aquarium, the dreaded Soviet GRU, the Red Army's Military Intelligence branch. It was after him that my boss had sent me, something that, I reflected, made far more sense from the Quadrille's point of view than accepting a tacit alliance with this new law-enforcement monster of an agency to which friend Marvin belonged.

I'm not going to recite here everything I learn about him from our files, but, although the subject was already in his fifties, he was worth ten younger men — therefore, I had to tread carefully. Knowing the Russian military mentality in depth allowed me to clearly perceive how Goliath would go about setting up the ambush. The first member of his team gave me no trouble, I killed him without him ever knowing it. It was a shot from almost three hundred meters, but the bullet split his forehead while he stood guard under a tree holding a submachine gun. As they were employing a tactic that was typical of Russian bodyguards, I knew that this individual was the first security checkpoint, and that he was referred to as the *spotter*. The *spotter* wanders around outside with a carbine, or submachine gun, guarding the entrance to the shelter where they keep the subject. Only that they had two *spotters* instead of one; the second one was stationed near the backdoor of the ranch and I also neutralized him with the rifle.

When preparing the defense of a shelter, true professionals are more concerned with defending the backdoors, so I entered through the main doors precisely because it was the least likely place for someone with experience to choose as a point of infiltration. However, before entering I paused to swap the long-range rifle — little less than a nuisance once inside the house — for the dead watchman's submachine gun. I checked it out, a Czech Skorpio VZ 61, making sure it was fully loaded. I set the selector in automatic fire mode before I slipped inside. Now I knew that if those outside were carrying submachine guns, the interior team would surely be using shotguns.

The first ones I would have to deal with once inside were the *prowlers*, they usually hunt in pairs and wander around the house while the object of their protection remains in the safest room, closely guarded by the team's leader: the *champion.*

I don't think I have to spell out for you who that was....

Chapter 8

NO TRUCE

The confrontation with the men lurking inside the house was no walk in the park, if you must know. Here things began to get complicated for me, but the experience also helped me to realize that I was not fooling anyone with Krista's supposed abduction, since now Kaminski knew that his wife had not survived the encounter and that I was at his ranch for very different motives than the ones I had initially mentioned to him. In this bloody business nothing is ever what it seems, you know. But that is to be expected. I have already spoken of Goliath's background and experience, and if the Russian colossus was truly proficient in the techniques of Military Intelligence, by now he must have had a clear picture of who he was really dealing with.

The opposition on the first floor was fierce, but not an insurmountable obstacle; operating alone, I always knew where the enemy was. They did not. The mobsters prowling the second floor had to be careful not to shoot each other down in the heat of the battle. However, on the second story I was not so lucky; there I was able to eliminate only one of them, but the second gunman surprised me with a shotgun blast that almost split me in two. Fortunately, the buckshot load embedded itself in the twenty-seven layers of armor plate that lined my Tac-vest. And despite the pain caused by the impact, I was able to turn the shooter into mincemeat with a sustained burst from the SMG. In it went half a clip of the .32 ACP rounds that the Skorpion fires, the American equivalent to the European 7.65 mm shell.

The silence that followed spoke volumes. Goliath could see at that moment that Krista's "kidnapper" was coming for him, not for his boss.

Not everyone knew, of course — I'm sure not even Kaminski himself — that Goliath's real name was Viktor Zotov. With the collapse of the Soviet Union, especially in the wake of the failed coup the hard-liners tried on Gorbachev, Zotov had fled Moscow and maintained a discreet profile until he was able to contact some of the emerging Russian Mafia clans in Helsinki. Top caliber enforcers are highly valued by criminal institutions, and finding a better one than the fearsome Red Goliath in those days was very difficult.

While reflecting about this, a savage howl (more like the roar of a wild beast) broke my train of thoughts as it echoed throughout the second floor and, suddenly, I had before me a furious Leo Kaminski wielding his twin axes, slashing out in all directions, as he kept on hollering while coming at me.

"Jesus!" I snapped, jumping backward.

I was forced to twist my torso to keep The Sower from dismembering me alive, but the sharp edge of one of his hatchets passed by a little too close to my left shoulder, drawing blood.

I yelled at the top of my lungs because the pain tearing at my wound was intense, and then I prepared to dodge his next attack. Kaminski was frantic, his normally shallow skin appeared flushed now as the all-consuming remorse spread over his face. With bulging eyes and bared teeth, Leo Kaminski bellowed curses, unintelligible to me, in his native tongue. However, despite the maelstrom of violence in which I was now immersed, it didn't take me long to grasp what was happening. If Kaminski was confronting me... who the hell was lurking behind?

The snort of the silencer marked the end of my doubts and of my evasive maneuvers. The impact of a 7.62 projectile — especially a subsonic one with a flattened copper head — is usually devastating. I know I cried out in agony and the pain that rushed through my body in a matter of seconds was one of the most excruciating sensations I have ever experienced. My right leg collapsed, and I fell heavily, bleeding from the back of my thigh and praying to God that the bloody bullet had not severed an artery. Then things got crazy. Zotov's second shot (which should have been for me) struck Kaminski's chest stopping his attack dead in its tracks. Once I understood what was happening, it did not surprise me — I would have probably done the same in the enforcer's place, although I would have finished off comrade Viktor first, without hesitation. But it seemed that the Red Goliath intended to save me for himself so that he could indulge in bragging. Blessed be human vanity! When I tried to turn around and return fire with the Skorpion, which miraculously remained in my right hand, Goliath kicked the Czech SMG away from me and returned to finishing Kaminski. His casual way of proceeding was an impressive display of that mastery that only old pros attain at the crowning of their craft.

Dead dogs don't bite, I thought, thus the briefcase

with the million dollars changed hands. Now Goliath was the new proud owner of one million dollars.

Zotov looked at me suspiciously for a moment, thought about it, and then gave me something to amuse myself with while he went to the pleasant business of getting his big paws on the ransom loot. He planted a huge shoe on my thigh wound and pressed down with his formidable weight.

The brutal cry that escaped my throat echoed throughout the entire house.

Chapter 9

WHEN WORDS BECOME SUPERFLUOUS

By the time I came to notice, Goliath was already back; his imposing silhouette, towering over me like the China wall — well, a Russian one — was holding the case with the money in one hand and his smoking Tokarev pistol in the other.

"Hello, Delta," he greeted me in a quiet manner that hid well all the rage he felt inside. "After so many years in the Cold War, it seems unbelievable how you survived only to die here, without glory, in a secluded ranch in Clewiston, at the hands of the only enemy agent you could never dispose of...."

There were two of them, meaning "the enemies I couldn't dispose of" from that now seemingly distant era, but this bloody spawn of the defunct Soviet Russia had no reason to know that.

"Don't think you fooled me, *amigo*. It was a crude farce on your part, your infiltration of Kaminski's gang by impersonating Buchinsky first, and then this fake kidnapping thing... You killed her, did you? That's what you were sent to do. I always suspected that it was you they would send to get me, the American assassin codenamed Delta, the most ruthless hitman in Col.

Berkowitz's unit... Ah, but your time has come, you swine!"

The hard-liners of the former Soviet Union were always noted for being very theatrical people, bent as they were on giving the impression of being invincible to the rest of the world. And comrade Zotov here was no exception.

"Damn you, Goliath!" I hissed through clenched teeth.

He eyed me carefully with grim determination, before saying: "No..., damn *you*, you pathetic Yankee. DAMN YOU!! Do you know how many bullets I owe you? A lot more than I have left in the clip of this gun. You should see yourself now, Delta, you are a pathetic sight, but I lost so many good comrades to your bullets in the past that I don't feel one iota of compassion for you. Sorry, *amigo*," he added, "end of the line."

Every word he ushered, every gesture he made, was aimed at reducing my will to fight back. But he made the mistake of moving closer, believing I was defeated. Of course, the picture was too tempting for a man like him to pass, a man whom I had shamed in the eyes of his superiors by eliminating the rest of his cell. So now he was rejoicing to see me broken and bleeding, splattered on the floor, while his huge, hairy body stood over me. I guess for Viktor Zotov it was the symbolism that mattered at that moment: Yankeeland about to be crushed under the Soviet boot. I know he had it in for me and all that, but when you are sent to tangle with old pros, such as yours truly, you never take chances.

The son of a bitch understood that too late when I kicked his knee from under him. Goliath let out a grunt of pain mixed with rage and shot me before his right leg buckled and he fell to the ground. He would have killed me too had I not anticipated his reaction, cocking my body to roll away from him. I let out an impressive bellow and threw myself at the Skorpion SMG that Goliath had kicked away from me. I wielded it, turned to him with unsuspected speed for a wounded man and emptied the rest of the magazine on him. Center mass, as the FBI boys call it in their shooting practices.

Just like I'd done that other time, almost fifteen years ago, during Operation Red Mushroom on the docks of Manhattan*.

*Refers to the first volume in the series, entitled *The Quadrille* (Author's Note)

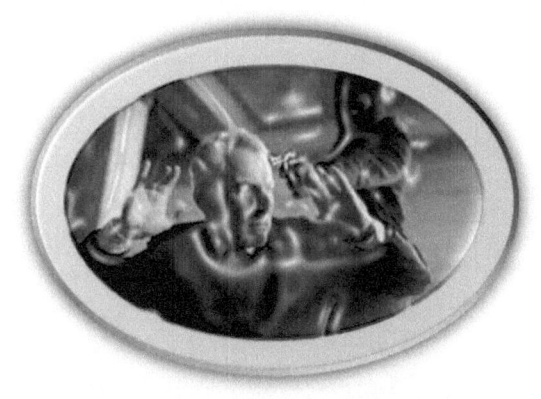

A DIFFERENT GAME

Part Two

*C*hapter *10*

BACK IN THE FOLD

Weeks later, while I was resting in a rented room at the Embassy Suites Hotel near the intersection of Le Jeune Avenue and Okeechobee Road, the Colonel stopped by to greet me and check on my health. It was good to see him again; during my stay at the hospital, I'd heard rumors that Alfred Tilson had also returned to the Quadrille and my boss confirmed them. Tilson was an ex-CIA master assassin who, for making one mistake (only one), had been kicked out of the Moscow Section and if he hadn't suffered any major setbacks in his career, he had Col. Berkowitz to thank for that, who promptly became his benefactor by offering Old Al a position in his new shadow unit, molding the new recruits into well-oiled killing machines.

"How are you feeling, Delta?" he asked, removing his hat and the raincoat he wore over his timeless steel-gray suit. The attaché case he carried in his right hand was left on top of the counter that separated the room from the kitchenette.

It was pouring rain outside, this was a facet I had not yet learned about the state of Florida; for some reason, we citizens from the rest of the Union tend to see Florida — especially Miami — as some sort of enchanted oasis where the sun always shines... Well, nothing is perfect.

"I can't complain, Colonel; happy to be alive. Nice to see you again, sir," I said and pointed to one of the velvet-lined armchairs that furnished the small living room. "Sit down, please, may I pour you a drink?"

Before accepting, my boss took a significant glance at his wristwatch and pursed his lips. It was a few minutes past two o'clock in the afternoon, although the rain descending over the city had darkened the sky. He was a man completely devoted to military discipline and consuming alcohol any time before six, with no apparent reason for celebration, was something that did not fit his stern personality.

"Ah, what the hell!" he mumbled. "Pour me one."

"You want it *puro*, or on the rocks?"

"*Puro*, of course." He answered.

"Very good, sir. One straight whisky coming up."

I couldn't suppress a smile: we were celebrating something — his reaction made that obvious now — whatever it was. Maybe it was Tilson's return, or maybe there were other things unfolding he hadn't told me yet; in any event, with so much rain outside sweeping away the sins of the city, it was an excellent occasion to get drunk together in that hotel room where we were under the shelter of a roof and four solid concrete walls on a fifth floor and there were no enemies roaming around; at least, as far as I could tell. It seemed like here we could afford the luxury of being human and vulnerable, again.

I poured his whiskey and handed it to him. I decanted myself one in the same measure and when I came to sit across from him, the Colonel stretched out his right hand with the now empty glass and surprised me by requesting: "Another one, if you please."

This time I served him a double and hurried to plop down on my chair. Something must have been burning his insides to feel the need of ingesting alcohol in such portions.

"You sure you're okay, Delta?" he inquired, looking straight into my eyes. The glass of amber-colored liquor held firmly between his hands.

"I'm fine, sir. Ready for whatever comes next. I have lost all the excess weight and sustained no severe injuries. The bullet that pierced my leg went through without, thank God, touching any major arteries or ligaments. The rest were painful scratches and lacerations of no consequence that I owe to the bloody hatchets of that damned Ukrainian mobster... Goliath only had a chance to shoot me; well, he also stomped on my wound. I lost a lot of blood, that's for sure, but I think the danger is past."

"In other words, you were *lucky*. In times of yore, when you were in peak condition, Zotov would never have touched you. Much less Kaminski."

I drew a long breath. "Perhaps... It is what it is, Colonel," I commented, raising an eyebrow, and pursing my lips in a casual shrug. "Nobody's perfect."

"Remember your first encounter with comrade Zotov?" his lips twisted into an intentional pout and the gleam that shone in his eyes told me he was recalling those days with pleasurable passion, the days when he'd recruited me for the Quadrille to clean the streets of Manhattan of all the atomic saboteurs of the former KGB.

I took a long pull from my whiskey and sighed. "Yes, sir. I remember." I spoke. "I know it was a botched job according to you and Tilson because I didn't finish him off when I should have, but my chest swelled with pride when I emptied the clip of my Hush Puppy on him and watched the big bastard go down, bleeding from chest and mouth, on the Manhattan Harbor pier. He put up

81

no resistance when I took away the briefcase with the last component of the bomb from him... The same briefcase with which he tried to crush my skull."

Evoking those glorious moments was a good therapy that strengthened our bond and made us smile in full satisfaction; drinking whiskey together had the same effect. The Colonel raised his glass to toast the good old times and the days to come. Hell, a dead and buried Viktor Zotov was something worth celebrating.

"How little did we know about the man when you almost killed him the first time in the Big Apple! We had no idea who the comrade really was."

"Landon pointed him out to me as an enemy agent who was linked to the pickup operations Yuri Pavenko was running on the pier, but he thought Goliath was just another illegal working for the KGB."

"Totally wrong," my boss pontificated, "Zotov had been loaned to the KGB for his expertise in introducing and removing secret components from the United States, but that was something the GRU people handled with better skill. Besides, his physical appearance harmonized well with the fake merchant marine image he projected."

"A gigantic merchant sailor was how Landon described him to me... Heck, can you imagine, Colonel, Landon, describing the guy as *gigantic*!

We both laughed, although it never was a laughing matter. But then if you knew Landon, at least the Landon I got to operate with back during those days in the Big Apple, I'm sure you could appreciate the irony a lot better.

"But you didn't flinch, Pat, 2+despite your youth and inexperience at the time. True, you were a crack sniper, and well-tested under fire, but you know damn well — Tilson will corroborate it — that it's one thing to kill from a distance and quite another to do it face to face, in cold blood," he said.

Listening to him start addressing me by my first name, and somewhat complimenting my past wanderings, made me think the whiskey was getting to him. I'd never had the opportunity to sit down and drink with him, so I had no notion of how far his alcoholic tolerance would stretch. I'd never known him to have a reputation as a drinker; therefore, it must not have been much.

"Now I want you to give me your account of the facts, I'm being pressured to turn in a written report, but I do not intend to do so because our position in the racket is not yet officially defined — if you know what I mean — and the individual who is asking for it is not entirely trustworthy..."

"Let me guess," I interrupted him, "Marvin's big boss."

"That's right. However, I do plan to bring Attorney General Woods-Renault up to speed... She's a political ally, and she's looking for a window to get us back in the fold. Besides, I do need to know exactly how things happened and although I already have a good idea based on Wilfred's recount, there's nothing like hearing it from the protagonist's mouth. Don't you think?

I drew a long breath and looked into his eyes; what I saw in them pleased me. The old fox was satisfied with my work, he just wanted to rejoice in the facts as he heard them from my lips.

"Yes, sir."

A couple of hours later, after telling him in detail everything that had happened since I killed Buchinsky in that alley in New Orleans, until I ended up in the contours of Lake Okeechobee shooting it out with the former Soviet GRU agent, I began to worry about the beatific expression that had been taking over my boss's face.

I'd never seen him smile like that before....

"Hey, are you all right, Colonel?" I asked, pointing with my right index to his glass of whiskey.

"Am I all right, you ask? Why, I'm better than ever! Pour me another one, damn it, neat and double."

His answer increased my apprehension, for the gent in front of me was one of the seven most dangerous men in the world, and his brain was crowded with lots of compromising information.

"Relax, Pat," he said with a wry smile and a sly look in his eyes, "there's nothing to worry about, everything is under control. We are celebrating our return, that's all."

"Our return. Yes, sir."

He raised his drink, and I imitated him.

"Long life to the Quadrille," he muttered.

"Long life, sir," I repeated after him and we clinked our glasses.

That night we got terribly drunk, but the next morning, the Colonel took off early, leaving me the attaché he'd brought with him. At first, I thought that he had forgotten it, since he left it exactly where he had placed it upon arrival: on the kitchenette counter. But I immediately dismissed the thought; my boss is not the type who "forgets" things like that, not even suffering from a nasty hangover. I tentatively opened it to satisfy my curiosity and stumbled upon an 8.5" by 11" Manila envelope, quite bulky, in fact, along with a file marked TOP SECRET in capital vermilion letters. In addition to these two items, in the green velvet false bottom rested a short-barreled revolver, two and a half inches no more. It was a Colt .38 Special with a metal shroud guarding the hammer of the gun, six shots in the cylinder and a box of fifty FEDERAL brand hollow-point cartridges. The shroud over the hammer was an ingenious innovation, to prevent the weapon from getting caught in the fabric of your clothes, when carried around in concealment. No badge, no holster, no batons or taser guns though that was to be expected. Hell, we are just a band of professional Government hitmen, not Keystone cops.

Chapter 11

BEG TO GOD

Beg to God and sharpen your axe...

So goes an old popular Viking saying that contains a lot of logic, like most popular sayings I have come across in my life. In this case, the "begging" had to be done by the Colonel with the new political connections he was establishing in Washington and I, of course, had been trusted with "the axe." At first, perhaps because of the rumors about Alfred Tilson's return to the Quadrille, I thought that old Al would be my partner in crime on the road I had to travel to straighten things out, but I was wrong. He was conspicuously absent during those first confusing days of reformation and if he was with us (or not) in the struggle to get our old unit reestablished, he kept pretty much to himself, or perhaps he was following other orders from our reckless leader that I never learned of. I knew for a fact that the Colonel always preferred to keep us apart to avoid personality clashes between us volatile characters and only on rare occasions, when there was no other alternative, did he risk pairing us up. Apparently, he'd seen no reason to do so now. Nevertheless, and because of the magnitude of what he had in store for me, I was again assigned the tactical support of our guide Wilfred.

The file marked TOP SECRET was nothing more than a flow chart with some dossiers pertaining to my next assignment. While I, to some extent, had neutralized the illegal marijuana trade organized by The Sower and disposed of The Butcher in the process — I leave out the elimination of Goliath because this particular goal only concerned my boss and his handlers from the DOD — I still had to tackle the illicit gambling ring of floating casinos that the late Leo Kaminski and his wife, Krista, had been setting up in the Florida Keys and stop another sinister character of international background who until that moment had been unknown to me. I'm referring to a Colombian criminal known as Rudy Cuevas, the alleged partner of the Kaminskis in the gambling operation.

According to the Colonel, The Sower's motive in choosing the costly services of Viktor Zotov over the two hardmen offered by Cuevas was particularly because in Goliath, Kaminski not only found the expertise of a super tough enforcer with military background, but also the experience accumulated over years in detecting and investigating U.S. military radar technology. The OCF and the Treasury Department had their sights set on Cuevas because, aside from being the most relevant foreign investor in the floating casinos, he had close ties to an elusive gang of counterfeiters from Santiago de Cali, who specialized in printing and smuggling large quantities of paper money: mostly U.S. and Canadian dollars. Cuevas was the middleman who moved the production of the clandestine printing presses from Colombia to the Florida Keys, where American and Canadian gamblers lost their bets in genuine dollars but got paid in counterfeit money instead when they lucked out... This — axiomatically speaking — had the Treasury boys foaming at their mouths. So vehement was their

obsession to find out how the hell were these Colombians getting their fake dollars into our shores that
they'd even requisitioned a USAF spy plane to patrol the
Florida Straits day and night.

It was to counter this measure that Leo Kaminski had
hired Viktor Zotov to neutralize the opposition; or at
least give it a try. If anyone had a chance to do so, it was
Goliath, whom The Sower respected for his presumed
contacts within the Russian Army. But the plan back-
fired on the Ukrainian mobster. Zotov, like many of the
old Soviet hardliners who finally traded the hammer and
the sickle for the green of our dollars, was no longer as
well-connected with the military apparatus of the new
Russian Federation, although it suited him to keep up
the charade before Kaminski for obvious reasons.

My boss, however, and his handlers from the Department of Defense, chose not to take any chances based on
comrade Viktor's reputation, and ended up sending me
to track down Goliath and — if he were back in the game
— put an end to the threat. That a renegade Soviet spy
could shoot down, or hijack, an E-3 Sentry class aircraft
to study the advanced radar technology these monster
planes carry in a mushroom-shaped dome mounted on
their fuselage was unacceptable in certain Washington
circles. And if the Treasury Department in its mad rush
to stop Cuevas did not mind taking such a risk, the
hawks at the Pentagon sure as hell did, and they made
their voices heard in the Department of Defense. No
former Soviet spy — no matter how experienced or
daring — was going to lay a hand on their AWACS
technology.

Period.

Of course, in the case of the Organized Crime Force,
the new law enforcement agency with global jurisdiction
that was being concocted to confront the Russian Mafia,

political or military reasons were not paramount (at least at that time). And that was why my boss was giving me *carte blanche* to cooperate with them again, even though our main objective had already been accomplished. The last paragraphs of the file he had left me were written in a most clear and direct language: I was to collaborate with Marvin and company in the dismantling of the floating casinos ring because the Colonel's strategy, at the time, was to impress director Feldman with the efficiency and dedication of the Quadrille so that he would feel "encouraged" to annex our small unit of *expendable* clandestine operators as one of the many divisions — more like a subsection in our case — of his vast mother agency.

Reading this, I refrained from cursing out loud and drew a long breath.

Well, we had to start somewhere.

As a plan to get our unit back on track it was an excellent strategy, but if I'm giving the impression of considering it the contrary it's because some tactics — no matter how brilliant they seem when you look them over on paper — never work well in the practice. There are times when the best schemes blow up in our faces and soon, we were going to find out that working shoulder to shoulder with Arnold Feldman's OCF, was not just a momentary table of salvation for the Quadrille but also a real time-bomb that could explode at any given moment....

However, as I said before: *Beg to God and sharpen your axe.*

*C*hapter *12*

ALLIES & ENEMIES

The historical center of Key West is not, as many seem to believe, the flashy docking facilities called City Marina, which is in Garrison Bight; *that* is its geographic center. The official one is a plaza known as Mallory Square. We arrived there in good time, as the appointment we had made with Marvin was not for another two hours and since we were terribly hungry, Wilfred parked his new car — I say new because on this occasion he was no longer driving a camouflaged cab — in the back parking lot of a McDonald's fast food restaurant and we set about the noble task of gobbling down hamburgers, French fries and a fascinating piece of apple pie. What can I say, I have a sweet tooth.

As we both happily tackled our lunch, I remembered that Key West had been the setting of a famous novel by Ernest Hemingway, *To Have and Have Not*, circa 1937, where he narrated the story of a local fisherman and a smuggler named Henry Morgan. It was not exactly a buccaneer and pirate adventure from centuries past, as the name of one of the characters suggests, but a drama out of the Great Depression era in the Florida Keys. However, the golden, aromatic presence of my portion of French fries interrupted my cultural musings, bringing my mind back to the delicacies of the American fast-food cuisine, which called for my undivided attention from their red little cardboard tray. Our lunch was complemented by a creamy chocolate milkshake, topped with a gleaming cherry.

Marvin had not been idle during all the months I'd been working undercover with Kaminski's gang. First — I noticed this as soon as we saw him — the guy had been working out in the gym. His shoulders and back were remarkably robust, his neck too, where thick veins stood out on both flanks that I hadn't noticed before (was he taking steroids?) This peculiarity gave him a more ominous and biting aspect than the one he had when I first met him. I remember that back in the Casino Royale of Nassau, Bahamas, he had the looks of a sophisticated gambler, dressed in what the English call *black tie*, while now he'd changed his aspect to a foul-mouthed Inspector Callahan of the San Francisco P. D. You may know him as Dirty Harry. But it wasn't only his physical appearance that had changed, there were other signs that were obvious to the judgment of the trained observer: the gnawing look in his eyes, for example, that exaggerated impatience one perceived in him and a furrowed brow at all times, as if at any moment he was going to pull out a goddamned .44 Magnum to blow your brains out with... *Go ahead, punk, make my day* and all that.

"I'm so glad to see you both here," he scowled entering the McDonald's like a thunderstorm and taking a seat at our table. "*At least* you are on time."

Wilfred gave me a sidelong glance, raising an eyebrow; he didn't seem to be comfortable with the commentary nor the corporeal language employed by Marvin, who was acting with unnecessary aggressiveness that seemed to be aimed at us. I didn't like it either, especially the consonance of that "at least." Marvin's dismissive accent hinted that neither my colleague nor I were on his list of valued people.

"This operation has been a disaster from the start..." he hissed, looking me straight in the eye. "Nothing went as it should have!"

Wilfred bit his tongue not to say anything. Or maybe he didn't understand what Marvin was referring to; the truth is, neither did I. As far as I knew my intervention in the matter had been quite successful, but then I remembered that, from the beginning, the objectives of the Quadrille were never the same as those of the Organized Crime Force. Even more reason for me to bite my tongue and prick up my ears.

"I never imagined that partnering with you two would derail us... Hasn't your boss told you what happened?"

Wilfred looked at me again, this time with some incredulity reflected on his dark eyes, and I could understand from his tense look and reluctance to utter a word, that the man was about to explode.

"All right, all right," I said to placate the spirits, "calm down, Marvin; as far as I know, our part of the operation has been a success. There is no more Sower, nor Butcher, nor even that giant Kaminski had in charge of security in Santiago de Cali: that Goliath guy. Those were my three targets, *amigo*, and I took them out. What's more, as a bonus, just in case she was able to pick up the pieces and put the racket back in motion again, I also got rid of Kaminski's wife. What is your grief?"

"I know, dammit, you did that after *kidnapping* her, *raping* her, and *demanding* a million-dollar ransom that, to this date, no one has been able to locate!"

I started to speak but stopped, then I noticed with some apprehension how my body tensed, and the memory of that karate chop he had hit me with during the little episode with the Colonel at the Opa Locka safehouse, ruffled the hairs on the back of my neck.

This was a bad sign, you know. *Very* bad.

On the verge of exploding, Marvin made a titanic effort to control himself. The muscles in his forearms tensed and the cluster of greenish veins that criss-crossed them swelled. They looked like a nest of sub-cutaneous snakes trying to escape through his skin. But he also bit his tongue and expelled the air contained by the rage that gnawed at his insides. It was beginning to look as if this forced ungodly alliance would end up giving us a heart attack....

Finally, Marvin drew a long breath and spoke. "The reason you were infiltrated into Kaminski's gang was so that, at the right time, you could assist the agent we already had in place in whatever was necessary."

"What?!" I cried out, dumbfounded. "Was there an OCF agent planted among Kaminski's gang?"

"God! Are you going to tell me you didn't know? Your boss was told! He must have told *you*! Didn't she ever give you the recognition signal we have for contact? She must have!"

"*She*...?" I asked, taken by surprise.

That came totally unexpected. Those were very hard months in which communication with home base had been virtually impossible without giving away my identity. However, I was tormented by the fact that the Colonel, knowing what had happened, had not prepared me for this meeting with Marvin. The truth is that I never suspected nor registered the existence of any OCF agent infiltrating The Sower's gang, much less a *female* agent. The only woman I had dealings with was... Aw, shit.

And that's when it all became clear to me. "Fuck..." I mumbled. "No way...."

Eventually, after spending many hours racking the

brain, one comes to understand the why of things, even if logic evades us for the moment by confronting reality in an untimely and crude manner. All law enforcement agencies work the same way: infiltrating agents or buying informants in the enemy's camp. What my boss should not have kept a secret was the real nature of this vast new organization to which he insisted on getting us attached to, so the Quadrille could get back into business. But I should have figured that all by myself; this was peace time, wasn't it? The Cold War was over, Federal law enforcement was the only path left to us — at least, for the time being.

I sighed and looked at Wilfred. My mouth was not moving, but my eyes told him: *We are fucked.*

I had taken for granted that an agency that would seriously consider annexing a shadow unit like the Quadrille had to operate under our same rules of engagement. The Nazis, in World War II, had a very appropriate name to define an outfit like ours, they called it: *Mordgruppe.* We were not in the business of arresting people or prosecuting anyone according to the standard international laws or justice, we never were, we were a team of eliminators exclusively dedicated to handling "wet affairs."

How the hell could I even imagine that those who tested us before making use of our skills intended anything else?

As expected, the meeting with Marvin did not end on a good note. Nevertheless, I tried my best to be fair to him (although I loathed the guy more and more with each passing minute) and reluctantly apologized for any detriment my lack of education might have caused. I ended by saying that I had no idea as to what had happened to the million dollars I'd asked of Leo Kaminski as ransom, but that if he didn't believe me that was just as well; he could follow up with my superior whenever he saw him. This slowed him down a bit; it was obvious that he respected the Colonel much more than he respected me, but in order not to lose face before us he said that he would contact my boss to clarify the situation at the proper time. For the moment, he was more pressed to close Operation High Keys and bust the gang of counterfeiters represented by Cuevas. He added that he'd managed to get the Colombians to travel to the Keys to inspect the site where the bales of fake money could be delivered and to assure the rest of the interested parties that the pipeline would continue to deliver in our shores without a hitch. Wilfred and I hastened to agree to meet him again the next day at an address he provided us, where the meeting with the South Americans was supposed to take place. Then Marvin vanished and I asked Fred to drive around looking for a public phone where I could make a call to the Colonel.

Minutes later I had my boss on the line.

"I don't like this one bit, Delta," I heard his voice at the other end of the connection, "Marvin is obviously obsessed with the mission. He must be neutralized."

Somehow, I had guessed that was going to be his reaction. For him, the world was very simple because he saw everything in black and white. You were either with him, or you were against him, as the Madison Avenue boys used to say in the old days. And Marvin didn't seem to be with us anymore.

"Neutralize him, yes sir..." I repeated into the earpiece with every intention to make him hear his own words from my mouth and think, again, about what he was ordering me to do. "Neutralize him how?"

He answered my question with a question: "You are calling from a public phone, aren't you?"

"Yes, sir."

"Give me the number to call you back in a few minutes. Don't go far and make sure the booth stays vacant until we speak again. Answer the call as soon as you hear the buzzer. You copy?"

"Yes, sir," I said and hung up.

I drew a long breath and looked hesitantly at Wilfred, who was leaning against the trunk of his car with his arms crossed over his chest and a contrite expression on his face.

"Don't worry, I don't understand it either. Right now, the Colonel is trying to decide the best way to proceed."

"You're wrong, Delta. I *do* understand what's going on, but it's best if the Colonel is the one to set a course of action for us. At the end of the day, mine it's just a hunch."

I looked him in the eye. "Would you care to share your hunch with me?"

"Sure," he said. "These bastards used us to wipe their asses and now we stink; that must be it."

I sighed: "I have a guess too... do you happen to know what friend Marvin's last name is?"

He squinted his eyelids before telling me: "His last name is Rosen... Rosen something..."

"Rosenberger, or Rosenstrauch?"

"Rosenstrauch! That's it! I heard it from his mouth by chance, but his credentials as an OCF special agent have him listed as Marvin Rose."

"Rose. It figures, many European Jews choose to modify their surnames upon migrating to America for the sole purpose of "Americanizing" them.... Marvin

Rosenstrauch... I'll bet one of my testicles that his family comes from Central Europe. Kaminski was a European Jew. The Sower was born in Ukraine to a Polish father and a Ukrainian mother, but Krista..."

"Krista was Polish?" he interrupted me.

"Not Polish, Fred, she was a German Jew — do you know what her maiden name was?"

Wilfred's eyes twinkled with the light of under-standing. "No, but I can imagine it," he whispered philosophically. "Rosenstrauch, isn't that it?

At that instant, before I had time to answer him, the ringing of the telephone echoed off the glass panels of the public phone booth, and I rushed to take the call.

"Yes?"

"It's me, Delta," I heard the Colonel say at the other end of the line. What he told me next confirmed all my suspicions; but, even so, with his consent and all, the course of action he laid out for us was one worth stopping to think about.

Not just once, but twice.

*C*hapter *13*

ALL THE PIECES FALL INTO PLACE

With the Gulf of Mexico westward of Key West and the Atlantic Ocean to the east, I reflected, if Rudy Cuevas and his entourage decided to make the trip from Colombia by sea, or even by air but in a private aircraft, it would be more convenient for them to approach by the western route. Key West does have an international airport, but if the counterfeiters chose not to be so obvious in case the DEA and the Treasury Department's brackets were tracking them, it was also possible to fly as simple tourists in a commercial airline jet to Miami and from there work their way by road back to the Keys. Certainly, a more prolonged journey, if you must know, but one with fewer complications. In any event, it didn't affect us in the least what route the bandits chose to get there. Marvin had given us a place and a time, and all we had to do now was be prepared to close the trap once all the "mice" were pooled inside.

Bloody easy, wasn't it? That's why I didn't buy it.

"How good are you with a long-range rifle, buddy?" I asked Wilfred as we drove leisurely down the Overseas Highway.

My partner watched me out of the corner of his eye for half a second before returning his gaze to the road and refocusing squarely on the traffic.

"Acceptable, but it's not my cup of tea; I lack the cold blood. Give me a submachine gun or a pistol and the tables turn."

I grinned. His answer fit: Latin-blooded Caribbean, explosive guy... *Rambo in Key West*, I thought.

"Yes, soldier. Nothing like the Marine Corps, huh?"

This time he gave me a killer stare that made me smile and my smile rubbed off on him.

"How did you know I was a Marine, you too?"

"Nah, I was with the Rangers. I just figured you for a Marine, that's all."

"What do you have in mind, Ranger?"

I grinned.

"Well, that's precisely what I want to talk to you about, but not on the road. I suppose you know the area well, don't you?"

"Sure. I'm the guide."

"Then you go find us a discreet place to drink a couple of beers, friend guide. We'll have that little talk there."

Fred nodded before saying, "Yes, sir!"

Earlier that same afternoon, after we had parted ways with Marvin Rose at the McDonald's on Mallory Square and had spoken to my superior on the phone, we were forced to retrace our steps and head north on the Overseas Highway, the Colonel's orders.

Our destination this time was the High Keys.

Having been alerted by me that there was trouble brewing with Agent Rose, Col. Berkowitz conducted his own investigation using his old Washington sources and other new ones who were joining our cause.

"I've been lucky, Delta," he said from the Opa Locka safehouse upon returning my call, "there's this young lady named Jessica Fitts; she's a redhead who happens to be an MIT graduate. She filled out an application for employment first with the FBI and then with the OCF last month but was flatly rejected by both agencies."

In all honesty, I failed to see the motive for the good fortune he was claiming to have; nonetheless, I refrained from saying so because the note of enthusiasm in his voice was quite high. This was strange in a man not at all comfortable with baring his feelings in front of subordinates. But this time, his optimism was showing, though I couldn't see why.

"MIT, sir? What the hell is that?"

He sighed at my blatant demonstration of the highest ignorance, but was very careful not to hurt my feelings by pointing it out, at least not that time, because our association was not yet official and much of the burden of the struggle to return to being the Quadrille now rested upon my shoulders... What can I say, even idiots have been known to be indispensable at some critical point.

"I'm referring to the Massachusetts Institute of Technology, Delta, MIT for short," he explained, "it's a private university in Cambridge with a great national reputation."

"I see, something like Harvard."

"More or less, but with some variations. The IQ required, no longer to graduate from MIT, but to be admitted as a student, is extremely high..."

"So that red-haired girl you mentioned must be a brain," I interrupted him, "and yet you say she's been rejected by both the FBI and the OCF. Why?"

He didn't answer that, of course.

"Someone brought her to my attention, and I took the risk of reaching out to her — I don't even know why I did it, I've never had analytical minds among the troops because it is counterproductive in this kind of operation.

When I give an order, I don't need anyone to analyze it, do you understand? I just need an agent to carry it out. I take care of the analysis."

"Maybe that's why she got rejected on both counts," I reflected, thinking how different the Quadrille's recruitment rules were from those of the FBI and the CIA, which, in the case of the Bureau, only hired law students and, in the case of the Company, just recruited the know-it-alls from the most prestigious universities around the country. I thought that Carrots — being so analytical, as per my boss — would be better off hooking up with Langley, our unit was a sordid swamp, not an enchanted blue lagoon for the privileged minds of the nation. The Quadrille was formed by agents of brawn and quick wits — not to mention unscrupulous entities. But I refrained from making any scathing comments that I might regret going forward. Something in the tone of his voice said he was determined to recruit this particular young lady.

Well, good for him.

Presently, the Colonel drew a long breath and said: "Times are changing, Delta, and whoever is not proficient with computers in today's world is at a disadvantage."

"I don't know shit about computers and I'm not doing so bad myself, sir," I said with the intention of stinging him a bit. "In fact, neither do you."

"True, but for a field agent to be successful in today's theater of operations, it requires analysts who can find and interpret the data used by the director of operations to organize the missions."

"*Touché*," I admitted and dropped the subject.

"Anyway," my boss went on, "I approached Miss Fitts upon noting her persistence in seeking employment as a field agent and I've been sounding her out, in case Mr.

Feldman decides to throw us a line on this one. She told me that Marvin, whom she seems to know from her previous interactions with the Force, well, the OCF, has taken the death of Krista Kaminski to heart." He paused briefly. "It turns out that this Krista character was his informant, she was his cousin too, and he'd managed to convince her to betray her husband... How does that grab you?"

I cursed under my breath and shook my head in exasperation.

"Christ! Too bad I wasn't told sooner. I bet he was in love with that tramp, too. Krista had a gift for driving men crazy, Colonel... Perhaps that's why I killed her."

"I'm sure it was the right decision under the circumstances; you were alone behind enemy lines and surrounded by dangerous foes. Carrying the extra baggage would have jeopardized the mission, not to mention minimized your chances of survival, but you should *never* have raped her, Delta, your mission didn't require it."

"I did *not* rape her, sir!" I hissed. "The blonde bitch provoked me!"

"I don't care what happened between the two of you; the mission was accomplished, wasn't it? But you've made yourself an enemy in the process who, if not neutralized in time, is going to spoil the *only* chance we have of becoming part of the mechanism."

That had been his way of telling me that, since I had muddied it up by taking sexual advantage of Krista, now it was my turn to clean up after my own mess.

"I suspect Marvin thought about replacing Mrs. Kaminski with Miss Fitts, but time ran out on him. The Colombians, faced with the elimination of The Sower and Goliath, have become very suspicious and they're determined to be the ones in control of the operation.

Certainly not Marvin, or someone from around here."

"Based on what you are telling me, sir," I pointed out, "I must infer that Agent Rose has infiltrated the gang?"

"It appears so, although it is not clear to me how he managed it. I don't think the man is fooling anyone with his shenanigans unless he is keeping an ace up his sleeve and planning to sacrifice a pawn or two in the game to prove his loyalty to the Colombians. And you have reappeared at *just* the right moment, see? Besides, he's got it in for you."

"Of course, the sacrifice *pawn* must be me; it makes sense," his ominous silence at my sarcastic remark confirmed it. Now I had a strong motivation for getting rid of Marvin in case I had ever harbored any hesitancy — which I never had.

Before ending the call, he gave me instructions which I set out to follow to the letter. Wilfred led us to a road intersection near the mangroves that surround Hawk Channel in Islamorada. There, in a nook on one side of the road, a pearly white Jeep Cherokee Classic was parked waiting for us. It looked like the latest model, but it might have been from the previous year, at that time they had not yet changed the exterior design; it still had the same rugged outdoors looks that increased its fuel consumption far more than necessary.

Fred stopped our car next to the SUV. My partner parked just in front of the Jeep, on the hillside bristling with green-painted mile markers, so as not to block the road with the tail of our vehicle. There are two hundred and three miles of road along the Overseas Highway, but at the sight of the man who stepped out of the Jeep everything around us seemed to vanish with his mere presence. He was a legendary character within our unit, who belonged to that convoluted cloak-and-dagger world that enclosed my past; I never thought I would see him again. Like Alfred Tilson, he was one of those old war horses who'd been with the Quadrille from the very beginning and a very important part of the operation even though he was not an eliminator. His name was William Johnson, but we all called him Bill, the gunsmith.

"Goddammit!" He hissed as soon as he laid eyes on me, "Patrick Coonan, weren't you flying cargo planes for the CIA, kid?"

Calling me "kid," despite my thirty-eight years at the time, was because Bill was already well into his old age; even older than Tilson and the Colonel himself, because those two were still in their fifties.

"Bill, what a surprise! The Old Man didn't warn me that it would be you..."

"Oh, you know him! The bugger enjoys keeping everything from us till the very last minute, he loves surprises," he interrupted me, making me laugh at the thought of the face my boss would make if he heard Bill the gunsmith refers to him as a bugger. But Johnson was like that, and knowing he was the oldest in our group he would take such liberties; although I suspect he only did it behind the Colonel's back.

"I had no idea you were back with us!" I told him. "I heard you'd retired."

"I did, yes. But I soon discovered that I can't stand so many hours of the day looking at my wife's face and putting up with her nagging. But enough of the chatter, boys; time is short. Let's get back to what we are all doing here, shall we?"

Bill let go of the hand he'd shaken and lifted the rear door of the cargo bay of the SUV.

"Here's everything you'll need to close your mission," he announced with a wink.

"Hey, Bill, do you know Fred?" I inquired as I realized

I hadn't introduced him to our guide yet.

"I haven't seen him before, but I've heard of him, Col. Berkowitz thinks highly of him. His name is Wilfred, isn't it?

"Wilfred," confirmed my partner and took a step forward to shake Bill's hand.

"I'm Bill. Nice to meet you, kid. If you've been partnered with Pat..."

"The code name is Delta," I corrected him.

"Sure, with Delta here, it's because you measure up," he went on. "Not many in our outfit can say the same."

He smiled and before any of us could retort, he handed the keys to the Jeep over to Fred and claimed our vehicle keys in return.

"Take care of yourselves, lads. I'll be in touch... Ah, Delta, I have a message for you from the Colonel.

"A message?" I frowned, "I just got off the phone with him, less than an hour ago...."

"He says, and here I quote his words verbatim, that no one should interfere with the axe, when it is busy chopping wood."

"Ah, yes, the axe... Very good, Bill. Duly noted."

At the end of our rendezvous with Johnson, Fred and I boarded the Jeep and he drove us back to Key West. When I asked him to find a place where we could have a few beers and a relaxed conversation, he nodded and pulled off to Duval Street. It's a very popular street in Key West and probably the only one in the entire Conch Republic where you can find just about everything; literally speaking. We left behind the old Strand Theater and a place called Captain Tony's Saloon, and continued down the street until we reached Sloppy Joe's Bar, another tavern just as noisy, but with the difference that it was here (so the story goes) where E. Hemingway had met his third wife. The walls of the place were witness to this, they are full of pictures with images of the time that spoke of the friendship between the great American novelist and the proud owner of that picturesque locale.

"What's on your mind, Delta?" asked my partner once we were seated at a booth for two and a solicitous waiter placed a pitcher of cold beer with two crystal glasses on the surface. The beer sat next to a small plate brimming with salted peanuts.

I drew a long breath and shrugged my shoulders. "There's not much to talk about, partner. The orders have already been issued. What I want to do here is figure out together how we're going to do this." I paused to grab a handful of peanuts and dump them in my mouth. "How well do you know the area where the rendezvous point Marvin gave us lies? I need to make sure of this."

"Well, I know it's a shipyard on Higgs Beach, which lies between Southernmost Point and the West Martello turret."

"Far away from here?"

"No, not far at all. In fact, it's at the end of Duval Street. All we need to do is take it southbound and we'll be there in a few minutes."

"All right, then that's going to be our stop once we leave this cantina."

"But Marvin did not schedule the rendezvous until tomorrow...."

"Precisely, the idea is to recon the terrain way before we show up there like a couple of meek pigeons. I guess you already guessed that it's a trap."

"You think so?"

"Hell, man, I'm *sure!*"

"You are sure of *what*, Delta?"

I stared at him grimly. "First of all, Marvin has it in for me about Krista, I just found out they were first cousins, and, besides, I suspect he desired her as a woman...."

"Seriously? Aren't you overreacting?"

I grinned. "You didn't know her like I did, Fred, she was a slut; she'd bed any man she liked or planned to manipulate at her convenience. Marvin is under the impression that I raped her, and he's been going with the gossip to Col. Berkowitz, but I swear it wasn't like that, it was her who provoked me! She knew I had the hots for her, sure, that much is true, but first and foremost I'm a pro. In other words, I don't tend to mix sex with work, mind you — at least not for personal reasons. That's partly how I have survived all these years."

"You have a good record," he admitted and raised his beer glass to his mouth, "when the Colonel let me know he was going to pair me with you, I asked to read your file."

I frowned.

"Did the Old Man let you?" I asked, astonished. "It's supposed to be a secret file."

"I know, but I don't like working with strangers and the Colonel didn't have anyone else with my skills at the time; he had to give in. But don't you worry, partner, your file never left the safehouse. He forced me to read it in his office, in his presence, and when I finished, he made me give it back to him."

I grinned. "Wow, Bill was right then, Col. Berkowitz thinks highly of you. He's never done that before."

"Back to Krista," Wilfred said, "what did she plan for you?"

"That's where the crux of the matter lies, until now I hadn't had time to think about it because of the speed with which the events took place, but I've already begun to see everything more clearly. I think she was trying to be clever. Use me for her purposes and then have me killed. She never gave me a recognition signal, I swear."

"That briefcase we brought back from the ranch when I rescued you, what did it contain, Delta, dirty money or secret documents?"

"A million dollars."

"Whoa! I should have kept it," he said wagging his head from side to side, as if lamenting his own stupidity, but I had him figured for an honest guy (over the years you learn to make them in the way they look at you; the scabrous ones almost never hold your gaze) and knowing my boss's marked tendency to recruit in military circles, chances were that Wilfred, was clean wheat.

"Be glad you didn't, kid; now that I know the rest of the story, I suspect it's all counterfeit money. You'd have gotten into a lot of trouble with the Treasury Department; I don't know if you know it, but they're after those dollars like bloodhounds after the fox. No matter how good the counterfeits are, the Treasury boys always find a way to detect them."

"You may be right," he grinned. "I handed the case with the money to the Colonel; I don't know what he did with it."

Of course, I didn't tell him that there was another case with twenty-five thousand dollars stumbling around somewhere; the one Krista had given me in that Mallory Square hotel where I had killed the two bodyguards, at her request.

"Going back to Krista and her ability to drive men crazy, she came to me one fine day when her husband was away and offered to become my playmate bunny for one whole week and twenty-five grand if I agreed to get rid of him, as well as the two men who were traveling with us. I was surprised by her proposal, because I understood she was sleeping with one of the bodyguards she wanted dead behind Leo Kaminski's back. It seems she was sweet-talking the sucker into doing the same thing she ended up asking of me."

Wilfred's eyes widened, but he didn't comment.

"The guy probably didn't have the balls to oblige her, and she changed her mind..." I went on. "After all, it didn't suit her to leave loose ends behind. People talk, you know. And there I was on hand, a professional killer with a great reputation up and down the East Coast, Dave Buchinsky, alias The Butcher. I often caught myself staring at her fanny and lusting after her body..." I paused to draw a long breath. "Hell, man, I made it easy for the bitch, it was her big break."

"Christ, the Colonel didn't tell me any of that," he muttered taciturnly after a few seconds.

"There was no need for you to know, *amigo*, it wasn't your mission. Your assignment was to rescue me and serve as my guide, only now things have changed, and I want to come clean with you. We're walking right into a trap, partner; both of us. Marvin is not going to bump me off and leave you alive so you can go to the Colonel with the details. Think about it."

"I'm thinking about it, man, but still...."

"If you prefer not to believe me, that's your prerogative, can't say I haven't had my doubts. But I've turned the situation so many times in my head that I'm utterly convinced. We're not going to make it out of that meeting, friend Fred, alive that is."

"Listen, Delta, for a crime to exist there's got to be a powerful motive — do you really think Marvin is going to throw you to the wolves just because of what happened with Krista?"

"I *know* he will! And there's another reason, too. He's planning on taking over the operation, therefore the need to throw a bone to the Colombians to be accepted as their new Gringo partner, now that the Kaminskis are gone. Marvin must gain their trust and keep the counterfeit dollars coming until that bloody AWACS plane pinpoints the spot where they smuggle the bales into the country, get it? They don't containerize them through the Port of Miami, that's for sure."

"The point of entry has to be Key West, no doubt about it," Wilfred backed me with conviction.

"It is, it must be. But where exactly...?"

There was an instant that the world around me seemed to coagulate; everything stopped in my mind and wham!

Suddenly, I saw it all clearly.

Chapter 14

THE MOUSETRAP

The Colonel's voice sounded rather skeptical over the phone, a bit over a hundred and fifty miles away.

"A submarine, you say... Now, really, Delta. Have you lost your mind?"

My boss stopped suddenly, because he probably experienced the same feeling of realization that I had only moments earlier when sharing the booth with Wilfred in the bar. It *had* to be a bathyscaph of sorts, or a midget sub; there was no other way.

"Listen, sir, can you locate that girl, the brainy red-head you told me about?

I heard him let out a gasp as he listened.

"I didn't know are you telepathic, Delta. I have her sitting in my office, as we speak, we were just talking about a job possibility. I imagine you mean Miss Fitts, don't you?"

"Yes, sir. Carrots, or whatever her name is, is she really in there with you?"

"What do you want with her?"

"Well, since she is an analyst and a computer expert, give her access to one and ask her to research and analyze the following... are you listening?

"Go ahead, I'll put you on speakerphone so she can listen too."

"I want Miss Fitts to look up the schematics of an E-3 Sentry spy plane, do you copy? This information is military and therefore should be classified, but if she really knows her stuff being a good hacker comes with the territory. Put her to the test, sir. I'll wait for the results."

"Very well," I heard my boss say and then he ordered Jessica to obtain the requested information. I guessed that by that time — more than a year had passed since I'd visited his office at the Opa Locka safehouse — my boss had managed to acquire a decent computer or two, perhaps an entire LAN network. Apparently so, because I immediately began to hear the distinct sound of dizzying typing over the phone. It didn't take long for them to come up with the information.

"Are you still there, Delta?"

"Yes, sir."

"Miss Fitts will read out loud to you what she has found."

Ipso facto, a young woman's voice with pleasant overtones, but still projecting a dour pitch, began to reach me.

"It's a Boeing 707 aircraft carrying a rotating mushroom on its back; the inside of this massive dome is packed with the innovative AWACS technology..."

"I know that, for God's sake, I want the schematics!" I interrupted her in annoyance. Actually, even the schematics was information I already had, but I needed the Colonel to hear it from other lips.

"This aircraft comes with a powerful APY-1 type Search Radar System, manufactured by the Westinghouse Company. This method has sufficient searching and tracking capabilities for a single E-3 Sentry to scan the airspace for six consecutive hours within a radius of 1,600 kilometers, equivalent to 1,000 miles. Twenty of these planes were successfully operated from Saudi Arabia during Operation Desert Storm…"

"Hold it right there, Miss," I interrupted her firmly, and, when her voice trailed off, I went on. "You see that, Colonel? If those Colombians were bringing in the bales in small planes or barges, the AWACS would detect it!"

"But how the hell do you think they've been able to procure a submarine, Delta? Not even the Colombian Navy owns one!"

I drew a long breath. "You are probably thinking about an attack nuclear sub, sir, but I don't think that's the case here. These guys are very ingenious, and they have money to burn; I think that what they are using in this instance are midget subs, like the Undersea Rescue Vehicles employed by our Navy — or a homemade type. Underwater mules if you know what I mean."

The absolute silence at the other end of the line seemed to indicate that my boss was beginning to accept my theory.

"Can you, please," I went on, "ask Miss Fitts to run a probe on midget submarines? There must be some information about their use in the drug smuggling trade, or maybe some military action by Colombian guerrillas in the Magdalena River basin… I think I read something about that."

"Miss Fitts," I heard the Colonel speak, "give it a shot, please."

Again, that furious whipping of keys came over the telephone connection. The Colonel cleared his throat a bit impatiently, it was not to his liking that a subordinate should take the lead in an operation. I could imagine the grimace of annoyance portrayed on his features as he struggled to save face in front of his brainy redhead. Just thinking about it made me grin.

"The *Ejército Nacional de Liberación*," said Carrots

after a few seconds, once she had stopped typing, "that's Spanish for the National Liberation Army, the most powerful guerrilla group in all of Colombia, has tried a couple of times to attack army bases on the Magdalena River. On one occasion, the ELN hijacked and modified an armored boat twenty meters long by three and a half meters wide, with capacity to carry forty men and sixteen assault guns..."

"There you are, Colonel, that's the precedent. I'll bet my neck that's what they're using: midget submarines. Withdraw the E-3, it's just wasting fuel and manpower hours. What is needed in this case is a frigate or two, possibly of the Knox-class that the Navy has lying around, unused, since they were taken out of service in '92. If I remember correctly, in the '80s they had forty-eight of them equipped with anti-submarine missiles that could hit their target within a ten-kilometer radius. That's what we need!"

I abruptly cut off the communication, leaving them — or so I hoped — as shocked as they were dumbfounded.

By the time I got back to our booth, Wilfred had already accounted for almost two thirds of the pitcher of beer. I downed what I had left in the one-trip glass and refilled it.

"Order another pitcher, if you want," I told him.

"So, what now?" he asked, looking me in the eye once the waiter had left.

On the table, between us, the new pitcher of cold beer stood like a crystal tower of golden transparency.

"They do it with a midget submarine," I commented with calculated composure, "or more than one. Maybe they own a small fleet of homemade subs. In any case, that's what we should be looking for, *amigo*: a midget sub."

"Gee, how cunning can they get!"

116

"Yep. Colombians are very clever."

"The abandoned dock makes sense then, that must be where they plan to dump the bales. The chosen spot must be located between Southernmost Point and West Martello." Fred spoke.

"Isn't that a strait frequented by tourism?"

"Not at present," he explained, "it was at one time. In the space between these two junctures lies Higgs Beach and the address Marvin gave us points to that area. The dock in question, as I recall, was owned by a local couple who were in the underwater photography business: the Greenbachs. *Oceanography Today* magazine used to hire them to take pictures of exotic corals and the local fauna, especially in Key Largo, where scuba diving is booming, but Adam died of a heart attack some time ago and his wife, Edna, didn't stay in the area."

"Who owns the property now?"

"I don't know, maybe Marvin bought it, or the Colombians through the Kaminskis. All I know is that the place is abandoned. Or looks like it."

"Or looks like it," I repeated after him, "I want to snoop around a little as soon as it gets dark."

"And the beer?"

"For the moment, drinking it all is our priority. Cheers."

"*Salud.*"

An hour and a half later, as the sun set, we boarded the Jeep and Wilfred drove in silence to the end of Duval Street; on the way south we passed Catherine Street, then United Street, and when we reached South Street — the last one before the hitting the ocean — we turned left and headed east.

We sighted the marina before reaching the West Martello Tower; it was a shady plank building with a rickety dock, its wooden structure bathed in the waters of Higgs Beach. The saltpeter and lack of maintenance of those days had gnawed at it like a hungry plague of evil termites. We hid the Jeep in the coastal brush and after loading the duffel bags Bill Johnson had left us with the weapons and equipment we needed for the job, we continued toward the dilapidated building. We were a pair of furtive shadows slipping into the darkness; our normal clothes had been replaced by night combat fatigues, dyed to blend in with the gloom.

I was carrying the same Colt .38 the Colonel had left me, it was loaded with six hollow-point cartridges. No silencer screwed on its barrel because (in real life) silencers do not work with revolvers — only pistols, rifles and submachine guns benefit from a noise suppressor — since they lack chambers that lock with a slide and instead of carrying a clip, they house their lethal charge in a perforated cylinder. The gases and the sound of the shot escape through the cylinder holes where the cartridges are loaded, not through the gun barrel. You only see "silenced revolvers" in fiction books and movies. Revolvers work with a double action firing pin, so they do not have a safety catch either — another common error among unexperienced fiction makers.

In the duffel bags we carried the heavy equipment, but we would get to that later, once we found a good place to dig in. It was necessary to explore our surroundings thoroughly before deciding. The plan was for me to stay outside the dock, in sniper mode, and send Wilfred alone to the rendezvous with Marvin to confuse the OCF man. When he asked why I was not there, Fred would tell him that the Colonel had ordered me to return to Miami urgently and leave him in charge of assisting Marvin in capturing the Colombians.

That is what we had agreed.

The counterfeiters, as I had guessed, arrived by land, considering that the road trip from Miami to the Keys (although longer) did not present great risks for them. And I say "them" because there were three men those who got out of the car: Rudy Cuevas (the boss), and the two *sicarios* that he'd offered Kaminski for protection and that The Sower had rejected because he preferred the services of Buchinsky and Zotov. Rico was the one of medium height and soap opera male star looks. Indio Billy, the behemoth who looked like a Hindu harem guardian. Oh, that motherfucker was *big*! Big and square as an industrial fridge-freezer. He had a round and expressionless face, with beady eyes hidden behind dark glasses. When I saw Cuevas getting out of Lincoln, he was the last one out, I experienced total disenchantment. I had expected a replica of the "Franz Sánchez" played by Robert Davi in *License to Kill* — or at least "Darío," Sanchez's henchman played by Benicio del Toro — but the third man in the entourage was little more than a bald pygmy with the torso of a wine barrel on a pair of frog's legs. He looked just like a grotesque caricature of actor Danny de Vito.

They arrived well before the appointed time for the meeting with Marvin, something I also anticipated. The night before, Wilfred and I had mined the dock with Bill's C-4 bomblets, a volatile plastic explosive of military ordinance that only had to be grazed by a shot to explode. With Fred at my side aiming his binoculars toward the Greenbachs' old mooring, I watched through the rifle scope following the three men as they inspected the contours of the dock carrying the firearms they had removed from the Lincoln's large trunk. Cuevas wielded a massive long-barreled .357 Magnum revolver in his right hand; Rico and Indio Billy were carrying submachine guns that resembled 9mm Ingram Mac-10s. Judging by the careful way in which they handled their choppers, the two Colombian hardmen seemed to know how to use them.

I grinned as I watched Cuevas move awkwardly with his massive handgun in his tiny puffy hands, playing at being *Dirty Harry*, and wondered if the little man had any idea how hard that monster kicked. They searched the dock without finding the bombs and when they returned to the car to confer among themselves, along came Marvin squealing tires in a black pickup truck. It was a Dodge Ram, mind you, a very powerful vehicle with lots of gleaming chrome on the front grill and fenders; it commanded attention. Next to me, Fred put down the binoculars he'd been using and reached into one of the duffel bags, pulled open the zipper and reached for the Skorpion VZ 61 SMG that I had confiscated from one of Kaminski's guards back at the Double K ranch. He inserted a twenty-round magazine, grabbed a spare clip, and tucked it in a pocket. As he was about to leave for the dock, I took him by the arm and pulled him closer.

"Change of plans, *amigo*," I whispered in his ear, "given the circumstances, it is not necessary to risk your neck by going to meet them, now that all the rats are already inside the trap."

He grinned. "Just what I was thinking."

"Find yourself a spot from where you can cover the access to the marina where they parked their vehicles. When I start shooting, anyone who runs in that direction is yours. Mow them down. All right?"

He didn't answer momentarily. I felt him draw a deep breath and then gradually turn to look me in the eye.

"Marvin too?" he asked in a low, fatalistic tone.

"What do you think, partner?"

He didn't have time to answer me, because it was at that instant that three burly men sprouted from the underbrush and jumped us.

Chapter 15

THIS IS THE QUADRILLE

They were not ordinary citizens; they had training. After the first blows we exchanged in their attempt to capture us, it became obvious that we were dealing with agents of the federal government; the great unknown that troubled me was which of the big agencies they belonged to: the DEA? the OCF? Or were they Treasury Department's men?

It got ugly.

The trio was determined to arrest us and when they realized that they had a tiger by the tail — well, two, because both Fred and I gave them a rough time — one of them tried to pull out a gun and I had no choice but to neutralize him. At first, I thought I was going to be able to stop him without killing him, then I realized that I could not. It was a tremendous fatality because the brawl was a two-way fight and if they were determined not to let us flee, we were even more determined not to let them capture us.

When the melee was over (without any of them firing a single shot) the three inert bodies of our assailants lay on the ground, while Wilfred and I, both bleeding and exhausted from the rigors of hand-to-hand combat, searched them conscientiously, stripping them of all their weapons and I.D. badges.

They were OCF people, I ascertained with some relief; the least we needed at this point was to antagonize the other two big sister agencies.

"Hell..." my partner grumbled under his breath, "where did these clowns come from?"

Then Wilfred disappeared into the undergrowth with the Skorpion clutched in his hands, very focused on not making noises. I too began to move around the outside grounds of the ramshackle property, looking for an inconspicuous spot where I could hide with a good view of the site where Marvin was meeting with the Colombians. I counted to ten, to allow Wilfred time to get into position, and then climbed a tree that had a thick limb on which I positioned myself and readied my rifle.

We heard them before we could see them, it was their angry voices in rapid-fire Spanish, Colombian style, that more than talking sounded as if they were arguing with each other. Soon I had them in sight: Marvin first, trying to calm the dwarf who seemed very upset, and then the bodyguards. The latter also appeared unhappy but refrained from interfering in the boss's discussion with the Gringo policeman; they just listened attentively and watched the contours.

I took a couple of deep breaths and emptied my lungs before accommodating the rifle butt against my right shoulder and bringing my eyes in line with the scope. Marvin's broad back appeared in the telescopic lens. He was wearing a two-piece brown suit. His head was shaking violently as he shouted and waved his hands in desperation. Cuevas was watching him closely; his expression was glacial, but his brow furrowed as he scrutinized the big cop with great suspicion; he didn't believe a word Agent Rose was saying. Slowly turning the scope to see what was going on with the others in the background, I watched as the one called Rico stumbled over what looked like a bulge protruding from the wall and his right hand clutched at that compact lump that had grazed him. When I focused on the bodyguard's hand, I could see that what he held between his fingers was one of the C-4 bomblets.

I didn't waste any time and took the shot.

The bomb went off, taking off his hand and a large part of his head as well. His decapitated body, spurting blood from the truncated base of his neck, fell backwards and bounced off the plank floor. Then Indio Billy reacted by firing a burst from his Mac-10 chopper in my direction, while Cuevas and Marvin ran for cover. A burst from another submachine gun of smaller caliber was heard and I saw the grotesque gorilla receive several bullet impacts that doubled him with pain, like in the old King Kong movies, when the monstrous ape is attacked by fighter planes in New York. I figured that, before concentrating on Cuevas and Marvin, it would be best to neutralize the hulking bastard, because I feared that the light .32 ACP rounds fired by Wilfred's Skorpion SMG would not be enough to stop such a giant of a man; Indio Billy ranked in the same league as the late Goliath, pound for pound.

I reloaded the rifle, fixed the crosshairs of the scope on the plexus of the massive slaughterman, and fired at the base of the neck, where the sternum meets the clavicles, just in case he was wearing a bulletproof vest. The couple of .306 caliber rounds I put just below his throat jolted him with double impact — well, it's a tender spot. I watched as his lips parted to cry out in pain and I knew I'd killed him as he fell heavily to his knees, watching in stupor as the blood spread all over his chest. I waited no longer; I dropped the rifle and swung from the tree. I ran as fast as I could with the Colt in my hand, ready to shoot anyone who got in my way who wasn't

Wilfred.

When I arrived at the dock, I noticed that my partner was already inside the berth, shooting it out with a desperate Cuevas and maybe even with Marvin too.

While Fred kept them busy with his Czech submachine gun, I was stealthily combing the interior of the dock, praying that a stray bullet would not provoke more C-4 bomblets detonations. I was thinking about how to put an end to all that, when the fire abruptly ceased.

"Marvin!" I heard Fred shout. "Stop shooting! I've got the midget, there's no one else left!"

For a few seconds there was no response.

I held my breath so I could listen better for any noises, however slight, that would give away the OCF man's position.

"Where is Delta?" Agent Rose spoke out. "He's the one who's been shooting with a rifle, isn't he?"

I was able to locate him before Fred answered and made a cautious detour that put me at his back while my partner told him: "No. Delta was removed from the operation last night. Colonel Berkowitz was not amused to learn that he blackmailed Kaminski by kidnapping his wife, plus the disappearance of the attaché with the million-dollar ransom provoked a reaction."

Score one for you, Fred, I thought, *always tell the enemy what he wants to hear.*

I heard Marvin Rose let out a gasp and stand up, he'd been crouching behind what was left of a decayed plank ladder where, as a matter of fact, I had planted another of the C-4 charges Bill Johnson had prepared for us. At the entrance to the dock, Fred's silhouette stood against the sunlight, escorting a grumpy Cuevas, who walked reluctantly in front of my partner, with both hands clasped behind his head. Wilfred held him at gunpoint with the Colombian's own long-barreled big revolver, while the light Skorpion submachine gun hung from a thin leather harness at his side.

When Marvin left his hiding place behind the ladder, he raised the barrel of a Glock 9mm and pointed it in their direction.

"Don't fuck with me!" exclaimed the OCF man walking very sure of himself towards my partner, but still pointing the Glock at him. Or maybe it was Cuevas he was aiming at, who knows; from my position it was hard to tell.

"Put the gun down, Wilfred. There's a madman out there with a long-range rifle, Coonan or not, make him give himself up or you're a dead man."

You will be anyway, Fred, don't indulge him. I thought.

That's when my partner suddenly assimilated the seriousness of his situation. However, he still couldn't make up his mind to shoot Marvin.

"Listen, man..." Fred spoke, "this is ridiculous, we're supposed to be players on the same team."

"Oh yeah? Seriously? And where are my three colleagues who were waiting outside?"

"Which colleagues?" I whispered to his back. "The ones you gave orders to ambush us and beat us to a pulp?"

It was useless to continue with the farce, Agent Rose was not going to let himself be conned and I began to think of an idea that might allow us to close the operation in a convenient way for the Quadrille, although the poor devil was not going to survive our methods.

"Let's end the charade," I said, leaning the barrel of the Colt against the back of his neck, "the party is over. Put the safety on the gun and hand it over to me. Careful, now. Hold it by the barrel and turn around very slowly.

I have a highly sensitive trigger finger."

I pushed his head with the Colt's barrel so he could feel the full weight of the threat and took a couple of steps away from him to give him some space.

He turned slowly and looked at me with hatred in his eyes and for an instant I feared that anger would block his good sense and force me to kill him right then and there, with my own gun; something I was not supposed to do.

"Hey, hey..., watch it! Easy, easy... Now, be a good boy and hand me that gun."

I took the Glock away from him, made sure the safety of the pistol was on, and slipped it into one of my night combat fatigues large pockets.

"On your knees, *amigo*. Hands on your head, come on. You need to calm down because we need to talk. We can't go on like this."

He had all the rage in the world portrayed on his face. His features were distorted by passion and anger.

"You goddamned murderer!" he spat between his teeth. "I'm going to take you apart with my bare hands!"

The funny thing about these guys who start telling you what they're going to do to you, is that they usually never succeed.

"On your knees!" I shouted and put a bullet very close to his position, without hitting him.

The noise from a .38 Special shot is deafening and impressive.

Marvin dropped to his knees.

"Hands above your head!" I roared and fired another close shot at him.

Marvin raised his hands. *This is the last bullet I'll waste*, I thought, I had four more left in the cylinder.

"Now you're going to listen to me, you bastard..." I hissed at Marvin before calling out to Fred. "Wilfred!"

"Here I am, partner."

"Keep an eye on Mr. Cuevas. Okay?"

"Got it."

I returned my attention to Marvin. "Listen to me good, *amigo*, because I'm only going to say it once: I *didn't* rape Krista. She was a bitch and what happened to her was well-deserved. As for this one..." I paused to point at Cuevas with the short barrel of the Colt, "he can serve us better alive. Watch and learn."

I looked at Fred and realized that my little speech had relaxed him a bit. His concern for Marvin's life — I could see — was gradually dissipating.

"All right," I said, "this is the best time to settle the matter."

I walked toward the Colombian and pointed my gun at him.

"Hand me the canon, Fred."

Wilfred obeyed instantly and handed me the monstrous stainless-steel revolver. I put away my .38 and wielded the big Magnum in my right hand. At gunpoint I walked Cuevas to the kneeling OCF agent, who now showed some confusion on his face. Well, the truth is that everyone was confused; everyone but me, that is. It feels great to have the upper hand.

I had Cuevas stop about six feet away from Agent Rose.

"Mr. Cuevas, I'm going to ask you some questions and I want the truth. Your life is at stake now, do you copy?"

The Colombian nodded anxiously.

"Is this man your partner?" I inquired pointing to Marvin.

"Not quite yet, we were negotiating..." the Colombian spoke. "Upon Kaminski's death I was forced to find a replacement and..."

"And you preferred to do it by corrupting a Gringo

cop, didn't you? Of course! We Gringos are very accommodating when there are greenies rolling under the table."

Cuevas fell silent after giving me a slight nod.

"What did this fella tell you, that he belonged to the DEA, or the Treasury Department?

"Yes! He said he was an agent of the Treasury Department, that he could help us cover up the smuggling of the counterfeit dollars..."

"And you believed him, of course," I interrupted him scornfully. "That man," I added before momentarily pausing to break open the Magnum's cylinder and leave only one cartridge in it before locking it back into place, "has been deceiving you miserably. The only one, listen to me, the only son of a bitch who can do that for you is *me*! You may call me Delta," I shook my head firmly and handed him the big revolver, butt first, while pointing with my head in Marvin's direction.

"He's gone as far as he can...."

Cuevas looked at me dubiously at first, he was won over by watching me reach for Marvin's Glock, pull the safety off, and point it at his head. When Marvin understood my game and roared like a wounded lion before attempting to throw himself at us, the Colombian goon reacted as I'd expected and shot him at point-blank range.

Wilfred also reacted by bringing the Skorpion in line to fire at Cuevas, but I waved him away. The poor guy was now more confused than ever. There was no doubt that working with me greatly affected his ability to act, but that's our job, dammit; nothing is what it seems when working the counterintelligence angle. *Nothing*.

Welcome to the Quadrille!

Before Cuevas could recover from the shock (I wasn't wrong in assuming that the little man had no idea how hard those Magnums kick) I snatched the smoking revolver from his trembling hands and pointed toward the dock's exit.

"Now you may leave, Mr. Cuevas. My partner and I will take care of cleaning up this mess. Go back to Cali, talk to your associates, and send those submarines full of counterfeit dollars to the Florida Keys; we will be waiting for them where you tell us to. The casino fleet will not operate from here, it is safer for us to do it in Fort Lauderdale. Here, take this," I paused to pull out a cell phone that Bill had prepared as part of the arsenal and handed it to a still-dazzled Cuevas, "saved in the memory of this gadget is a phone number. Use it only to contact me when the cargo is on its way, got it? Now, get lost."

The Colombian grabbed the cell phone and slipped it into his pocket. He looked into my eyes at length and then nodded.

"Don't forget," I grinned, "the codeword is Delta."

"Sure... Delta," he repeated in a low growl. Thereupon he turned around and vanished.

I approached Wilfred slowly, taking care not to make any sudden movements that would appear threatening to him. The adrenaline of combat was still coursing through his veins, and the last scene he had experienced at my expense was not a very reassuring one, was it? He must have had a very low opinion of me.

I drew a long breath and spoke.

"You're still young and if you don't like what you've seen, maybe you should think about changing outfits. But if you decide to stay with us, get used to it, my friend: this is the Quadrille."

He didn't answer me. After a few seconds he lowered the SMG and let out a sigh.

"Come on, *amigo*," I said in an affable tone, "we've

got work to do...."

We invested some time in lifting the corpses of the three men we'd left hidden in the bushes and dragging them inside the dock. To leave a credible scenario for the Key West authorities, with Marvin's pistol (yet unfired) I sprayed the corpses of Rico and Indio Billy with 9mm slugs; Wilfred did the same using the weapons of the three agents who'd attacked us in the bushes and even fired a few random rounds at the walls.

After that we just got the hell out of there.

*E*pilogue

Several weeks later after being placed on standby by my boss, the Colonel summoned me back to his office. He was still occupying the Opa Locka safehouse, but that would not remain so for long. In some strange way (and I say "strange" because after that first disastrous operation in the Florida Keys, where four of his special agents died for nothing, I never thought the annexation of our group to the OCF was still possible), Arnold Feldman had agreed to incorporate the Quadrille into his organization not as a full division, but as a sub-section, and a new headquarters especially designed for us was being arranged in Midtown Miami. It was then, for the first time, that I learned of the acronym CI5 — from that moment on, that would be the official designation of our new unit.

One of the pieces of news Col. Berkowitz gave me that afternoon was that Wilfred had resigned his position as a local "guide" with the Quadrille — well, CI5 — and was now working for the DEA. Aware of the man's Latino roots (and Spanish being, in fact, his first language) the Drug Enforcement Administration had gladly accepted him into their ranks and sent him over to Mexico as part of a team of American advisors collaborating directly with the Mexican Federal Police. I felt happy for Fred, he was one of those lads who, like the Boy Scouts, sees everything in black and white. Ah, good versus evil — what a romantic notion! But in the world in which we operate the means always justify the ends and there is no white, nor is there black.

The world is gray, friend Wilfred, the world is gray....

"The last good piece of news is that Miss Jessica Fitts accepted my offer of employment. She will start with us as soon as we move into the Midtown building that has been assigned as our new headquarters." The Colonel added. "In the meantime, I have sent her to Langley, to take a training course in field work."

"Field work! I thought you said this girl was hired as an intelligence analyst, sir."

"That's right, but our unit is too concise to afford the luxury of having analysts and field agents. We should all be capable of doing a bit of everything here, no regard. Upon her return, Agent Fitts will become your official partner..."

"What?!" I burst out.

He grinned at my despair.

"That's the price we must pay for reassuming our official status within the Homeland Security apparatus: modernizing. The federal government, specifically the Department of Justice, has a protocol we all must follow to the letter, Delta. At least, for now. As you know, we are no longer under the Department of Defense, like we used to be. In Arnold Feldman's OCF all agents must work as a team. If I don't pair her up with you, I'll be forced to find you a male partner and send you to the FBI's Academy in Quantico to take a course in IT and Computer Science as well... How does that grab you?"

"Shit!" I mumbled under my breath, but I'm sure he heard me. Marlon Berkowitz ignored me, of course. I would have killed him right there, not once, but a thousand times, instead I bared my teeth and let out a grunt.

"What's that, Delta?" he asked with a certain cool aplomb.

"Nothing, sir." I answered promptly. "Whatever you say."

"That's what I thought." He concluded and spent a couple of seconds extracting his briarwood pipe and filling the bowl with apple-scented tobacco from a black leather pouch.

"Oh, there's one more thing." my boss went on once he got the pipe going, "and I do hope that *this* makes your day. The tactic you employed at Higgs Beach worked out marvelously."

Hearing that made me snap my head up and shake the bad mood off.

"What do you mean, sir?"

The Colonel grinned and spoke. "Your wise recommendations to the Treasury Department had the desired effect: They returned the AWACS plane to the Air Force and called in the Navy. It was, in fact, a three-midget sub fleet the Colombians were using, Delta. And all three of them we sank. Now the Knox frigates can rest in peace and give way to their replacements. But at least two of them will go to the boat graveyard having wreaked havoc with their torpedoes on the enemy. After seeing what those old artillery barges have accomplished, I'm seriously considering requisitioning one for our exclusive use...."

I took this as a joke, of course, but with Marlon Berkowitz you never knew. The Old Man might have been quite serious.

"Unfortunately, the million dollars you took from Kaminski was all counterfeit and the Treasury boys confiscated it to study the prints. Now they are hell-bent on sending a team of their best agents to Colombia to search for the printing plates, but that is not going to happen in the time being. You see, they have no authority down there unless the Colombian government directly asks for our cooperation through the standard diplomatic channels. Something that may, or may not, happen sometime soon..." He paused, flashing a mischievous smile at me.

"In any case," my boss went on, "I have already informed the Attorney General that the agent who turned the tables on the counterfeiters in Key West has returned to my ranks and is *active* and *available* if she needs someone with brains and plenty of experience to operate incognito in Colombia."

The smile he flashed at me gave me the creeps.

"With all due respect, sir," I mumbled looking him in the eye this time, "you can go screw yourself."

As always when it does not suit him, he chose to play deaf, of course, so as not to be forced to discipline me. However, my spontaneous protest didn't do a thing to stop him. Eventually, I was sent on assignment to Colombia but certainly not after a band of simple counterfeiters, if you must know.

But that is another story.

THE END

ABOUT THE AUTHOR

OSCAR ORTIZ was born in 1959 (Matanzas, Cuba), but he was raised in the United States. From an early age he showed a talent and appreciation for art and literature and (to the same extent) a dislike for collective sports, business, science, and math. He spent his youth studying Commercial Art & Advertising. Ortiz is the winner of the "Sole Second Prize" in the **2006 ENRIQUE LABRADOR RUIZ INTERNATIONAL STORYWRITERS AWARD** with his crime story *La culpa fue de Hammett* (Blame it on Hammett) and was selected as a "Finalist" in the **2006 TELEMUNDO WRITERS WORKSHOP** contest. He has worked as a freelance screenwriter for Telemundo Puerto Rico and Cubana de Televisión Studios in Miami. He currently resides with his wife in South Florida.